Death at Presley Park

Elly Grant

Death at Presley Park

By **Elly Grant**

Published by Author Way Limited through CreateSpace
Copyright 2013 Elly Grant

This book has been brought to you by -

Discover other Author Way Limited titles at - http://www.authorway.net Or to contact the author mailto:ellygrant@authorway.net

Death at Presley Park is a work of fiction written by Elly Grant. No characters or events in the book are real and any similarity to people and events living or dead is purely coincidental. All rights reserved.

        ISBN-10:   150529715X
        ISBN -13:   978-1505297157

Death at Presley Park

Prologue

September 29th

They tumbled like rats out of a sewer, clawing and clambering as they slid down the slope desperate to escape the gunman. Men and women falling, tripping over each other, mothers dragging terrified children, losing their grip then attempting to swim against the tide to retrieve them, chaotically moving on instinct. Unable to comprehend what was happening, they stampeded, each of them thinking they were about to die, stumbling over the fallen, trampling on faces, crushing fingers, abandoning friends, in a desperate bid to survive.

Do you sometimes wonder how you'd behave in a crisis, if your life was on the line, if you were facing imminent death? Would you stop to help a stranger? Would you save your wife, your husband, your parents your children? Perhaps a mother would shield her child, but perhaps not.

This particular picnic in the park was anything but. It was mid-afternoon. A sultry, September sunshine bathed the sweet smelling, freshly cut grass with an orange hue. Women chatted about this and that, comparing children, cooking, clothes. Men played ball, drank beer, made plans to go fishing while children ran about squealing and chasing each other in an endless game of tag. The gunman, dressed in combat gear, walked purposefully to the middle of the grass, amongst the groups of families and friends, amongst the blankets on the ground, the remnants of fried chicken, sandwiches, cakes and soft drinks. No-one looked at him or acknowledged him, too busy interacting with their families or friends. He didn't look out of place as many people were clothed in fancy dress costumes. He could have been invisible and he wondered if he was. Smiling to himself, he was eerily calm, but his heart was racing, wired by the drugs he'd been popping all through the night and throughout the day to help him stay awake. Raising his automatic weapon he pirouetted, finger on the trigger, firing indiscriminately into the crowd, whooping and cheering as people collapsed dead and dying. It's just like the fairground, he thought.

"Where's my prize?" he muttered.

Before he could spin around again, those who could stand, who weren't already dead, injured or frozen with fear, were up and running, and the gunman, heart pounding in his chest with the thrill of it all, pursued them. He was no longer simply spraying a crowd of easy targets. The chase was on. The gunman felt adrenalin rushing through his veins, his rapidly beating heart pounding in his ears. He was now a hunter and the panicking, fleeing people were his prey.

TWO WEEKS BEFORE

CHAPTER 1

"What time are we meeting up with Bee and Johnny?" Mandy called as she fiddled with her hair. She was trying to get it just right and one cowlick simply wouldn't lie down. She sprayed on more hair lacquer. With her eyes smarting she began to cough as the cloud of gluey droplets engulfed her. "Damnation," she spluttered. A tear escaped over her eyelid threatening to make her mascara run. Quickly, she pulled a tissue from the box on the dressing table in front of her and carefully dabbed at her cheek. Then she heard the doorbell ring.

"Sitter's arrived," Theo called. "You've got ten minutes then we really must leave."

Mandy rose from her dressing-table stool and stood at the full length mirror for one final look. Then, brushing her hands over her hips admiringly, she grinned at her image, checking her teeth for lipstick smears. There's nothing more off-putting than facing lipstick stained teeth when you're trying to eat, she thought.

"Are you good to go? I'd like to arrive on time for once." Theo's irritation was clear as his voice boomed up from the bottom of the stairs. He didn't used to get irksome. He used to make jokes about Mandy's timekeeping, or lack of it, but now everything she did seemed to annoy him. Mandy didn't care she was bored with Theo and his pettiness. After twelve years of marriage she'd expected more from him.

She could have married anyone. All the boys had fancied her, helplessly drawn to her flashing eyes, luscious lips and curvaceous figure. With her blonde hair, she looked like a young Marylyn Monroe and, whilst there were lots of pretty girls at her school, many of whom would easily put out for a bottle of cheap wine and sweet words of undying love, Mandy was different. She fascinated her classmates. She had mastered the knack of making the boys think there was a chance of a sexual encounter whilst keeping them at arm's length. She was the prize they all desired and every one of them would have turned cartwheels to impress her. But in the end she chose Theo because he was the most popular boy in school, sporty and clever his family came from the wealthiest part of the suburbs. He was also tall and handsome, with a broad, lean frame and even features.

They became the golden couple, the pair everyone envied, the ones everyone else wanted to be. Mandy and Theo married as soon as he finished university. As an accountant he was a good earner and their first home was a small semi-detached in an upmarket suburb. Coming from a poor background, Mandy felt as if she'd won the lottery. Their son Charlie was born a year later and now they lived in a four bedroom detached in the best street.

"If you don't come now I'm leaving without you. I can't be late for this dinner. I'm going to the car and I'll only wait five minutes then I'll be off. You can get yourself a cab."

Oh shit, Mandy thought. She knew he wasn't making empty threats. Grabbing her bag she quickly made her way down the stairs in time to hear the front door slam.

"Bye Charlie, Bye Annie," she called to her son and the sitter then she practically flew out of the door. Theo had already reversed out of the driveway and, as she approached the car, he was revving the engine, itching to be on his way.

"So what's this dinner all about? What's so important that we can't be five minutes late?"

Theo was tight-lipped, he inhaled deeply before answering.

"I told you before," he said, his voice full of frustration. "We're dining with Carlo and Carlotta Donatelli. He owns 'Delectra' and we're trying to get signed up as a supplier. If Johnny can pull this off we'll be sitting pretty for the next three years. There're not many companies able to guarantee work for the next three weeks these days. That's why we can't be late. We're hosting the dinner. They're our guests."

"Who else will be there? Will it just be the six of us?"

"Donatelli's accountant Phil McKay and his wife Jean will also be there. It's important that you and Bee keep Carlotta and Jean entertained while we talk business. We can't afford to fuck this up. We don't want to lose this contract."

Mandy was disappointed. She'd been looking forward to spending time with Johnny. They'd met up twice now without their respective partners knowing and Mandy couldn't keep her hands off him. Who would have thought that Johnny Rigby, the class clown, would turn out to be a business genius? All the time she and Theo were living what they thought was a golden lifestyle, Johnny Rigby was wheeling and dealing and becoming a multi-millionaire. To think she'd turned down his proposal in favour of Theo. You live and learn, she thought wryly. Anyway, she reasoned, now she could have her cake and eat it. Now she'd have both men under her thumb.

Mandy and Theo barely spoke during the journey to the restaurant. He was occupied with thoughts on strategy for the business ahead, she with thoughts of her liaisons with Johnny Rigby. She'd dressed to impress tonight knowing that his wife could never compete. Even if Bee was dressed in designer gear and she wore a bin bag, Mandy would still be more glamorous, more alluring. She knew she'd just have to snap her fingers to have all the men in the room at her beck and call.

Johnny had already planned for them to spend a whole weekend together. In three weeks time his wife and her sister were going to Prague for the sister's birthday celebration. Theo was being sent to Birmingham to represent the company at a trade show and Charlie was going camping with the scouts. Mandy didn't know what their affair would lead to, but for the time being, the attention Johnny gave her and the feeling of power she held over him were enough. She wasn't quite ready to give up on her marriage just yet. Not until something better, something tangible was being offered. Who knows, she thought to herself, maybe she could do even better than Johnny. She was the wrong side of thirty now, just, but didn't look a day over twenty-five. There was still plenty of time to secure an older man with money, lots and lots of money, and maybe a chateau in France or an island in the Caribbean, someone super-rich, a billionaire perhaps. Sex was power and power led to wealth and Mandy was the queen of sex appeal, she had it in spades.

"Mandy, Mandy," Theo's words cut through her daydream.

"Wwhat?" she stuttered.

"I asked you to get out and guide me into the parking space. It's a tight fit for a car of this size. If you don't get out now you'll not have room to open the door."

"But it's starting to rain," she protested. "Couldn't you drop me right at the door then go and park? It took me ages to do my hair."

Theo sighed. He didn't want to have to put up with Mandy whining all evening. She could put a damper on the entire meeting if she didn't get her way. With pursed lips showing his annoyance, he put the car into gear and pulled forward at speed, braking hard at the entranceway. Mandy was thrown forward, the seatbelt locking her to her seat.

She scowled, struggling to free herself. "I'll see you inside," she said leaping out of the car and slamming the door behind her. "Asshole," she muttered as she straightened her dress.

"I hope you're not talking about me," a voice from behind her said and she spun round to see Johnny. "I've just been out for a smoke," he explained holding aloft his silver cigarette case.

"Oh, hi Johnny, of course I'm not talking about you. Theo makes me so mad sometimes. Where's Bee?"

"Not close enough to see this," he replied slapping her bottom playfully. He glanced at the front door to check Theo wasn't about then, grabbing her round the waist, pulled her towards him and kissed her passionately on the lips, his tongue exploring her mouth.

Mandy returned the kiss then quickly pulled away looking around furtively. "If you carry on like that we'll get caught," she hissed.

"It's the risk of being caught that heightens the passion. You know you want me. I bet we could sneak out during the meal and no one would notice. My car is parked in a dark corner of the car park. How about a romantic fuck between the main course and dessert? You could be my dessert," he added with a leer.

"You're incorrigible Johnny, you know that. Don't even think about it. We'll soon be spending a whole weekend together. We can't risk being caught, it's far too dangerous. You are a very bad boy," she added smiling and wagging her finger at him.

"But you love danger and you can't get enough of this bad boy," he replied, licking his lips suggestively. "Theo, hello, I'm just briefing this lovely gal of yours about Donatelli and his wife."

Mandy hadn't noticed Theo walking towards them and she was startled when she realised he was beside her. She hoped he hadn't overheard any of their conversation.

CHAPTER 2

Prior to arriving at the restaurant Johnny and his family had all been at home.

Johnny heard laughter coming from the lounge as he came out of his dressing room and he made his way towards it. He sauntered along the wide, bright corridor and smiled to himself as he gazed out of the floor to ceiling plate glass windows which made up the whole of the exterior wall. The views across the countryside were spectacular and he marvelled at the way his wife Bee had known instinctively how to instruct their builders in order to get the most out of their home. Everything from the on-suite bedrooms to the covered, solar heated swimming pool with its retractable roof was designed to the highest standard. He was good at making money, but Bee knew how to spend it wisely.

The laughter intensified as he approached the room. Sitting at the table with a board game set up between them were Bee, Emma aged ten, her six year old brother Alex and Marie the au-pair.

"But Alex you can't go backwards even if it would let you pick up the book of wisdom," Emma protested, her intense, hazel-coloured eyes showing her frustration. "Tell him Mum. He doesn't understand that it would be cheating."

"I suppose having a book of wisdom might have helped in this situation," Marie said smiling.

"Yes," Bee agreed. "I'm sorry, Darling, but Alex is just too young for this game. It's designed for players aged ten and over and he's just a little boy. Why don't you get something else like Hungry Hippos?"

"I hate that game. Alex is too rough," she whined. "I wish he would hurry up and grow up."

Johnny, who'd been watching from the doorway, looked admiringly at his pretty wife and beautiful children. Bee was petite and slender, she had even features and a fair complexion framed by soft brown curls. She was kind and gentle and she seemed to have a fragility about her that made Johnny, and every other man she came into contact with, want to protect her. When their children were born he couldn't believe how well she'd coped, delivering them with hardly a whimper, proving she was much tougher than she looked. He shouldn't really have been surprised as all through their married life she'd been strong, organised and in control. She ran the household in a relaxed but disciplined fashion and the children felt safe and confident with their well-ordered routine.

"Hello Darling," he said as he planted a kiss on Bee's cheek. "As usual you look beautiful and perfectly dressed for the occasion. "Hello little chickens," he said addressing the children. "Hi Marie," he acknowledged the au-pair. "We'll have to leave in about ten minutes. We're meeting Theo and Mandy at the restaurant."

Bee stood then went to gather up her coat and handbag. As she walked towards the door Johnny couldn't help comparing her to Mandy. He lusted after Mandy but he loved his wife. How fortunate he was that Mandy had turned down his proposal when they were younger or he might have been stuck in a stressful, loveless marriage with a scheming, high maintenance bitch. Instead he was blissfully happy with this undemanding, wonderful woman who was the love of his life. He could have Mandy, or a dozen other women just like her, any day of the week, but only Bee could truly have Johnny.

Their feet crunched on the driveway as they walked towards the Lexus. On seeing them coming, Colin, Johnny's driver immediately leapt out of the car and opened the passenger door for Bee.

"Good evening Mrs. Rigby. How are you this evening?" he enquired politely.

Bee climbed into the car and Colin raced round to open the opposite door for Johnny without waiting for her reply.

"Looks like rain this evening," Colin said as he got into the driver's seat. He turned on the ignition and snapped his seat belt closed.

"Thank you for giving up your evening off to drive us," Bee said. "I do hope Caitlin didn't mind." Bee liked Colin. The young man was tall and lanky and he had a cheeky smile. He was bursting with youthful enthusiasm and although they looked nothing alike, there was something about him that reminded her of Johnny when he was younger.

"No problem, Mrs Rigby", Colin replied. "We're saving up to buy our own place so I'm glad of the overtime, besides, Caitlin's working on a paper all weekend. It's to be ready for Monday. She's studying to become a paralegal. I'd just be sitting in front of the telly with her mum and dad. Trust me, I'd rather be working. There's only so much 'Britain's Got Talent' a person can stand."

Johnny cleared his throat indicating this line of conversation should end. He wanted to discuss the evening ahead with Bee and didn't wish to waste the entire journey listening to small talk between her and his employee.

Bee took the initiative and began, "Don't worry about the restaurant. I've arranged for us to have the small private area at the back. It's still in the main room. There's no solid door but the archway separates it from the rest of the flow of people and it's very discreet. I've asked the front of house manager to bring in some extra lighting with a couple of standard lamps so that you and your guests can see to read any relevant paperwork. I'll look after the wives and I'll make sure Mandy doesn't drink too much. We can't risk her flirting with our guests and becoming the floorshow."

"I just hope Theo is on time tonight," Johnny replied. "I've a couple of things to discuss with him before Donatelli arrives."

"If he's late it'll be Mandy's fault. Everything is always about her. She has no respect for anyone or anything," Bee replied bitterly.

The edge on her voice was tangible. Johnny felt a cold chill run down his spine and a jag of fear. Did Bee know something about him and Mandy, he wondered? It was just a bit of fun, it meant nothing to him. Mandy meant nothing to him. Bee noticed the frown lines on his forehead and she leaned over to kiss him lightly on the cheek.

"Don't worry, Darling," she said. "You'll be magnificent tonight and everything will be fine. Emma has informed me she'd like to have riding lessons and she wants you to buy her a pony and Alex would like a helicopter to take him to school. So you'd better secure the deal. Our children have expensive tastes."

Johnny laughed, "When I was Emma's age I wanted a bike but we couldn't afford one. Now she wants a pony and our six year old wants a chopper, and what about you, my love? What do you want?"

"Only you, Darling, don't worry, I want only you," she replied smiling.

Johnny returned her smile. He took her hand in his and gave it a light squeeze then he settled back in his seat and relaxed. She suspects nothing he thought and he breathed in deeply with relief.

CHAPTER 3

After he dropped Mr. and Mrs. Rigby at the restaurant Colin drove off in the car. Johnny told him to be on call, but said he didn't need him back there until ten-thirty so he had three hours to kill and he didn't intend to waste a moment of it.

After he and Caitlin got married, it seemed like a good idea for them to move out of their rented accommodation and in with her parents. It was a kind and generous gesture on their part to offer the young couple a rent free home. It meant they could save up to buy their own place, a chance to step onto the property ladder. Caitlin's mum and dad weren't difficult people to live with, quite the reverse in fact, but they were around all the time. Colin and Caitlin never had any time alone and having rented a place for over a year they were used to their own space.

He worked every hour God sent. Driving all week for Rigby's and also manning the switchboard of a local taxi company three evenings a week, filling in as a back-up driver if someone was off sick or on holiday. Caitlin worked for a legal practice in the town while at the same time studying for her exams. She was also an 'Avon' lady which enabled her to earn a bit extra every week. They weren't work shy and were saving like mad, but even still, finding a deposit of ten per cent plus the other costs involved would take them over two years, and all that effort would allow them to buy only a one bedroom apartment.

Colin was buzzing with nerves and excitement as he glanced at his watch. He didn't have much time, but if the traffic wasn't too heavy he'd make it. His plan seemed so simple but nevertheless he ran over the details in his mind once again to think it through. He constantly checked his watch and when the opportunity arose he drove down the back streets to avoid traffic lights. Arriving at Rigby's at seven-forty he pulled the car round to the warehouse.

"Yes! Made it," he said aloud. Twenty minutes until close of business, he thought.

Colin carefully parked the Lexus out of sight of the offices just in case someone was working late as he didn't want to be seen. Then he walked briskly to the warehouse reception.

"Hi, Eddie," he said to the store manager as he entered.

Eddie was thin and muscular, bald at the front with a greasy looking pony tail, held in place by an elastic band, dangling down the back of his dirty neck. He was in his sixties and thought he looked cool, like an aging rocker. He'd worked for Rigby's since the company first opened.

"Hello, Colin, you're working a bit late tonight. I thought I saw the Boss' car. Is everything okay? Is he coming in here?"

"No sweat, Eddie. He's waiting in the car. We're in a hurry."

"What are you looking for? Do you want me to fetch something for you?"

"If you don't mind Eddie, I'll go through to the store and find what I want. I know exactly what I need and I can locate it quickly. Just write me up an order for ten blu-ray recorders. Put it through as a corporate gift for Delectra. The Boss is dining with them tonight. You should see the restaurant. I just left Mrs. Rigby there," he said changing the subject. "The place is very luxurious. One course would probably cost me a week's wages. It's just as well my Caitlin can cook. We'd starve if we had to pay restaurant prices."

"That's right, rub it in Colin. At least you've got a wife to cook for you when you get home. I'm dining 'a la' Gino's Fish and Chip Shop. Mind you, when I retire I'm going to spend my life in Spain or on the golf course. Not being married any more has let me save quite a bit and I'll have my pension."

Colin was fidgety, he was aware of the minutes ticking away. Finally Eddie said, "Okay, you go on and get what you need while I prepare the paperwork."

Colin walked through the swing doors and quickly located the box he wanted, knowing exactly where it was placed in the store as he'd searched for it the day before. Checking the code number, he picked up the brown, corrugated carton then returned to reception. Eddie smirked when he saw the younger man struggling to manoeuvre back through the swing doors with the large box.

"Do you need a hand with that? Would you like me to carry it to the car for you? I see you don't go to the gym very often."

"I get all the exercise I need at home, thank you very much. Some of us are married," he added with a wink.

"Aye, vacuuming and washing dishes builds up a lot of muscles," Eddie replied laughing then he handed over the paperwork for signing. Colin scrawled a mark that could have been anything then once again he checked the time. Ten minutes to get into the car and leave before the second shift clocked off for the night.

"Gotta go Eddie, the Boss will be having a fit. I'll have to drive like Jensen Button or we'll be late."

With the box securely in his grasp he hurried to the car. His walk was laboured and disjointed as he struggled with the large package. Opening the boot, he hoisted the box in. His fingers were puffy and red from his exertions and when he jumped into the driver's seat to start the engine, his hands were trembling. Eddie was standing at the entrance to the store as Colin drove off and, as the vehicle passed him, he waved. Thank goodness the car had tinted windows, Colin thought or it would have been obvious that the boss wasn't with him. He couldn't help grinning as he drove away. When he sold the blu-rays it would certainly boost the house fund and no one would be any the wiser.

After seeing the car drive off Eddie returned to his desk, picked up the receipted paperwork and kissed it. He'd suspected the younger man would be in too much of a hurry to actually read what he was signing for and he'd been right. Now Eddie had an approved order for twenty blu-rays when only ten had in fact left the store. I'll need to put that right, he thought to himself and he smiled as he mentally went through the list of people who'd be receiving one for Christmas this year.

He felt justified in stealing from Rigby's. He'd known Johnny Rigby's dad, they'd grown up together, they'd been friends. Now Tommy's wide-boy son was treating him like a servant. When Tommy died it was Eddie who'd helped arrange the funeral. His pal would be turning in his grave if he saw the way Johnny was disrespecting him. He'd given everything to this company, never missed a day's work, putting in ten hour shifts, seven days a week at the beginning. And what did he have to show for it? His wife left him and he hadn't had a pay rise in five years. Now the little shit didn't even get out of the car to acknowledge him, sending a boy with the order instead.

Colin drove like the clappers, racing down side streets, praying no one's cat would be strolling across his path. He reached home before eight-thirty, easily enough time for the second part of his plan. He'd telephoned Caitlin on route, she was looking out of the window when he pulled up and, as he stepped out of the car, she signalled to him that she'd be two minutes. He raced round to the boot lifted the package and carried it to the garage where he hid it amongst the pile of furniture items he and Caitlin had stored there. By the time his wife emerged from the house he was back at the car.

"Wow, I bet this car cost as much as a house,"

she said, running her hand over the sleek paintwork. "Are you sure it's okay for us to go for a drive? Your boss won't mind?"

"As long as I'm back at the restaurant to pick them up and we don't go too far away in case he calls, we can do what we like. I thought we could drive down to the coast and stop at the smart restaurant on the front. We can splash out and get coffee and dessert. Then I'll bring you back here and I'll still be in good time to collect the Rigby's. What do you think? Would you like to do that?"

Caitlin's blue eyes shone, her pretty face lit up and she grinned like an excited child.

"I love you Colin Anderson," she said and she threw her arms round his neck and kissed him. "You know I love you, don't you? Mum and Dad think the world of you too."

And with my new way of making money we'll soon have our own place and I won't have to put up with them for much longer, he thought.

CHAPTER 4

"Why don't you toddle off and see Bee, there's a good girl," Johnny said.

"Yes, off you go, Darling. We'll follow shortly," Theo added.

Mandy felt miffed at being so summarily dismissed. She looked from one man to the other for any sign of weakness that would allow her to stay in their company. They both smiled benignly at her, stopping just short of patting her on the head and treating her like a precocious child, before turning and beginning a conversation which clearly excluded her. With no other choice she strode off, her heels clacking on the tiled floor of the lobby.

By the time she reached the dining room she'd managed to regain her composure, fix a strained smile on her face, then allow herself to be led to the table by a very young, skinny waiter whose suit seemed to be wearing him. As she walked through the archway Bee immediately stood up to greet her.

"Mandy, hello, my, don't you look fabulous tonight? How are you? Is Charlie well?"

The two women exchanged polite small talk then with the formalities out of the way, Mandy asked, "Have you met the Donatellis before? Do you know what they're like? Are we likely to be bored out of our minds this evening?"

"I've never met them and they might bore us to death, but as we're here to support our husbands, we'll just have to grin and bear it. This contract is worth a small fortune and Johnny's determined to pull off the deal."

"Well if the wives are dull we can always gin and bear it," Mandy replied attempting to make a joke.

"Ladies, good evening, so nice to see you again Mrs. Rigby," the wine waiter interrupted. "Can I get you an aperitif or perhaps some champagne?"

"No thanks, Henri, we'll wait until our guests arrive. This is a business meeting so we'd better keep a cool head," she added, looking pointedly at Mandy. "We'll just have a jug of iced water with lemon for the time being, please."

Mandy was about to protest, but when she saw the determined look on Bee's face she changed her mind, remembering all too sharply that Bee was the boss's wife and she was merely his bit on the side. Bitch, she thought, you won't be so smug if I steal Johnny away from you. I'll certainly be ordering champagne then.

As the minutes ticked by the women chatted, enquiring about each other's children, holiday plans and such like. They were running out of small talk when Mandy noticed a tall, handsome man standing a short distance from their table talking to the head waiter. He had fine, sculpted features and was elegantly attired from his head to his highly polished shoes. Everything about him shouted money. Every inch clothed by an Italian designer.

"I bet that's Carlo Donatelli," Mandy said to Bee. "My God, he's handsome. I wouldn't kick him out of bed."

"I wouldn't invite him into my bed in the first place," Bee replied, obviously irritated by Mandy's inane quip. "I'm perfectly satisfied with my own husband," she added.

For a split second Mandy was drawn up tight, wondering if Bee had any inkling about her and Johnny, but dismissed the thought almost immediately.

"Come on Bee, you know what I'm like," she replied. "I'm a hopeless flirt. I don't mean any harm. It's just a bit of banter."

"Well perhaps you should curb the banter tonight. This is a very important business meeting and we're only here to represent our husbands," Bee replied shortly.

Mandy smarted at the rebuke, but pursed her lips and kept quiet, once again feeling acutely aware of the differences in their positions.

The man was shown to their table and both women stood to greet him.

"Mr. Donatelli, I presume," Mandy said stepping forward and offering him her hand before Bee could say a word.

"Actually, I'm Phil McKay," he replied. "Are you Mrs. Rigby?"

"Actually, I'm Mrs. Rigby," Bee said stepping forward forcing Mandy to move aside. "This is Mrs. Walker our accountant's wife," she added dismissively.

"Please call me Bee. Do come and sit down. My husband should be in shortly he's probably having a cigarette outside," she added and she led him to the table ignoring Mandy completely.

"I met him outside. He was with Mr. Walker and he's indeed having a cigarette. I left Carlo to join him and I brought our wives inside. Carlotta can't stand Carlo smoking. She's just gone to the 'ladies' with my wife Jean to freshen up. They'll join us in a minute."

"Theo stopped smoking when I became pregnant with my son Charlie," Mandy said trying to become part of the conversation. "Do you have children, Phil?"

"No," was his short reply. "Excuse me for a moment please. I'll find out what's happened to the ladies." He stood and abruptly walked towards the door.

"He's a bit of a cold fish," Mandy said.

"Do you think so?" Bee replied. "I thought he was a perfect gentleman."

...

Apart from Jean and Carlotta the ladies room was empty. The two women chatted as they touched up their makeup.

"What an odd couple the guys from Rigby's are," Carlotta said.

"I know," Jean added. "Johnny's such a barrow boy and his associate talks as if he's got marbles in his mouth. I wonder what their wives are like. I hate these occasions, don't you? I hope our men finish their business negotiations early then we can go on to a club."

"Me too, but until they do we'll have to put up with the wives trying to impress us, it's such a bore. At least we should get a good meal here. I've heard Andreas Bellini is the chef."

"You look like you've been poured into that gown, Carlotta. Are you sure you'll have room to eat?"

"Don't be fooled, Jean. Everyone thinks that models just pick at their food. I eat like a horse. In fact, I'm so hungry I could eat a horse."

The two women couldn't have looked more different, Carlotta being very tall, standing six feet in her bare feet, with skin the colour of ebony and a stunningly beautiful face. She was rather shy, and although she turned heads wherever she went, modestly, she was always surprised to receive compliments. In contrast, Jean stood only five feet tall, had a slightly plump figure, a round, rosy-cheeked face, and whilst a smile was never far from her lips it was usually mocking or cruel. Unlike Carlotta who was kind and gentle, Jean could be as hard as nails and very judgmental.

"Oh well, into the valley of death," Jean said, and, with a final glance at their reflections, the women headed for the dining room.

Mandy was the first to notice when they entered.

"That has to be them," she said. "The tall black girl is probably Phil's wife, the short one Donatelli's. Italians are usually short, but Phil is really tall.

"The tall girl is very striking don't you think," Bee said.

"I suppose so, if you like that sort of look. These long-limbed, black women all look alike to me. Don't get me wrong. I'm not prejudiced. She is stunning, but I prefer an English rose type myself, that's all."

The women were shown to the table.

"I see we've all lost our husbands," Carlotta said. "Why do men always wander off?"

"If it's any consolation, Phil arrived then left again, the others haven't made it through the door yet," Bee replied then proceeded to make the introductions.

Mandy was surprised to discover that a handsome man like Phil had such a homely looking wife and she wondered what Donatelli would be like. Having such an attractive wife he was probably an Adonis she thought. She didn't have long to wait to find out because a couple of minutes later all the men came walking towards them and Mandy chuckled to herself at the sight of Carlo Donatelli. She couldn't have got it more wrong. He was tiny, not much taller than Jean McKay and fat, waddling rather than walking. His face resembled a dimpled cushion giving him the appearance of an overgrown baby. He wore so much vulgar gold jewellery on his pudgy fingers and round his fat neck he looked like a 1980's cliche. Oh dear, Mandy thought to herself, this is going to be a very long evening.

CHAPTER 5

Now that everyone was gathered at the restaurant, Bee began to chew on her lip nervously. Although she'd hosted dinner parties umpteen times, she had never before entertained such high profile guests. Carlo Donatelli was often in the press either for his business achievements or his generous charitable donations and his wife represented one fashion house which, if as successful as predicted, would propel her forward to super model status. Bee was acutely aware that the eyes of other diners were upon them and one young woman actually came forward to ask Carlotta for an autograph before being steered back to her own table.

Bee worried about the choice of food being wrong, the white wine not being properly chilled, the red wine not having enough time to breathe, who should sit beside whom, and more importantly, who shouldn't be seated next to Carlo. Even before they were settled at the table, she noticed Mandy gulping down champagne. Fortunately, her worries about the seating were unfounded though as the men positioned themselves in a huddle at one end of the table leaving the women to chat at the other end. With clever manipulation on Bee's part Mandy found herself placed at the last seat and she was not happy. She didn't want to talk to women all evening and really wanted to be sitting beside at least one man who wasn't her husband.

Johnny and Carlo slid into easy conversation chatting and laughing and before very long they discovered that their business backgrounds were very similar.

"Just like you, Johnny, many people resented my early success. They were jealous of me and didn't realise how hard it had been for me to reach my goals, but they didn't want to put in the graft, the sixteen hour days, seven days a week. They expected money to fall into their laps and couldn't understand when it didn't. I rarely see any of my old friends now. We no longer have anything in common."

I find the same thing," Johnny replied. "I've got good people working for me, but in the end, everything is down to me. No one else would go that extra mile."

"To be fair, I can't take all the credit for Delectra, the earlier companies yes, but not Delectra. Without Phil, who's been with me from the beginning, the company wouldn't be trading at this level. He's more than just my accountant he's my friend and a junior partner as well."

"I had no idea. I thought you were Mr. Delectra. The media never mentions Phil."

"We prefer it that way, although if you look up the structure of the company on-line you'll very quickly see the important role Phil plays. He's a business genius and he's the man to convince about the contract. I deal with the public image, but he's the man with the knowledge. He tells me what I can and can't spend and keeps up to date with what's happening in the worldwide market."

"I had no idea," Johnny repeated and he was sorry now that he wasn't sitting next to Phil. He just hoped Theo was up to the job of selling Rigby's services to him.

Bee played with the food on her plate while her guests ate every morsel of theirs. The more Mandy drank the more nervous Bee became until she could stand it no longer. She prodded Mandy's leg under the cover of the table and signalled for her to join her then she stood, excused herself and made for the ladies room, Mandy hot on her heels. When Mandy entered the room Bee, who was standing to the side of the door, shut it and leaned against it stopping anyone else from entering.

"What's going on? Are you feeling okay?" Mandy asked.

"I'm up to high doh, I'm completely on edge. This deal is the most important opportunity Rigby's has ever had and you're drinking for Britain. I want you to stop drinking before you make a fool of yourself and us. We're not yet on dessert and you've already consumed half a bottle of champagne and almost an entire bottle of red wine. I've only had one glass, the other women are drinking white wine and our bottle's empty. Whatever are you thinking of?"

Mandy's face was scarlet, but not from embarrassment, she was livid. How dare Bee criticise her. Who the hell did she think she was? Then she remembered how important this deal was for Johnny and she relented. When the time was right she'd crush

Bee like a bug. Everything comes to he who waits, but for the moment she had to toe the line and do as she was told. Mandy felt her eyes well with tears of frustration. Noticing her getting upset, Bee stood away from the door, grabbed her by the arm and marched her over to the wash hand basin.

"Don't you dare cry," she instructed. "I can't have you going back in there with red eyes and a tear stained face or they'll think you're some sad, old lush. I'm going back to my guests now. Pull yourself together then follow me. And remember, no more alcohol."

With that said Bee left the room and, as the door closed behind her Mandy clenched her fists, stared at her image in the mirror and gave a silent scream.

When Bee and Mandy first met the Donatellis they assumed Carlotta had married her diminutive husband because of his money and power. Neither could comprehend the beautiful and much younger woman finding anything else attractive about him, but they were wrong. Within a few minutes of speaking to her it was clear that Carlotta adored her husband. She found his short stature and pudgy body cute and she said that when he whispered words of undying love and passion to her in Italian, she couldn't imagine anything sexier.

"The very first time I saw those sad, puppy-dog eyes looking at me full of longing, I wanted this man," she said. "We were at a charity function and when he approached me and offered to get me a drink, I thought he was a waiter," she laughed. "The place was full of young men who were showing off and making lewd suggestions to me and there was my Carlo patiently fetching me champagne and canapés. I had no idea who he was and thinking he was working at the venue, I handed him a tip. He was completely dumbfounded. Because he was shy, it took him until almost the end of the evening to explain who he was and ask me for a date."

"And did he accept the tip?" Mandy asked.

Carlotta laughed, "Of course," she replied. "That's why he's so successful. He'd never turn down money. He still picks up pennies off the street, you know. He puts them in a jar and once a year gives the money to charity. Carlo's favourite saying is 'look after the pennies and the pounds take care of themselves'."

"He's probably the most generous man I've ever met," Jean added. "Generous in spirit as well as with material things. And he's incredibly kind."

"It's good of you to say that, but you're opinion is biased. The four of us have been friends for years," Carlotta explained. "Jean and I are as close as sisters. She's always there with good advice when I need it."

"Yes," Jean agreed. "An older, wiser sister, much older I'm afraid," she added with a wry smile.

"Do you and Carlo have any children?" Mandy asked. "I know from Phil that you two don't," she said turning to Jean and ignoring the warning glance from Bee.

A concerned look passed over Carlotta's face as she fixed her eyes on her friend. She looked as if she was about to make some comment then pursed her lips thinking better of it. Bee was annoyed with Mandy for mentioning it. The earlier shortness of Phil's reply to her enquiry about children should have been enough for her to realise it was a touchy subject.

After an awkward pause Carlotta said, "Carlo has two sons from his previous marriage but I have no children."

"Oh, was Carlo divorced when you met?" Mandy asked.

Bee stared at her darkly, "I'm sure that's none of our business," she said.

"It's all right," Carlotta replied her stern expression belying her words. "Carlo's first wife died of cancer. He was a devoted husband and he nursed her for two years. Both his sons now live in New York and before you ask they're not much younger than me."

"Excuse me," Jean said. "I'm just going to freshen up." She stood and headed for the toilets.

"Change the subject," Carlotta said to Mandy speaking softly but sternly. It was an order not a request. "Jean had seven miscarriages before having to have an emergency hysterectomy. She doesn't want to be reminded of her loss." Then she too stood and left the table.

Bee's jaw dropped, she wondered how Mandy could be so stupid and insensitive.

"What?" Mandy said noticing her incredulous stare. "I only asked. I was just making small talk. It's not my fault these stuck-up women are so touchy."

Sitting at one end of the table opposite Theo,

Phil McKay grilled the younger man rigorously. He wanted answers about every aspect of Rigby's business. Engaged in conversation with Carlo, Johnny could only look on helplessly. Eventually, noticing his discomfort Carlo said, "Why keep a dog and bark yourself."

"I beg your pardon?"

"I said why keep a dog and bark yourself. We both have our accountants here with us. They're the men who understand the numbers. If the deal looks good on paper then we'll be going ahead with our arrangement. If not, you and I will still have had an enjoyable evening and hopefully be able to leave the door open for another time." Carlo smiled benignly, his pudgy cheeks dimpling. "I hear you're holding a charity event at the end of the month," he said changing the subject. "Tell me about it."

From his seat Johnny could see that Theo looked strained and exhausted, but he could do nothing to assist him. He hoped and prayed he wouldn't let him down. If he could pull this deal off, Johnny would owe him big time.

After nearly an hour Phil closed the small, leather-bound notebook he'd been writing in and placed it in his inside jacket pocket along with his gold, Cross pen. He reached forward and picked up his glass, "This really is an excellent wine," he said, sipping the robust Burgundy. He looked as fresh and alert as when he'd arrived. By contrast, Theo slumped in his chair. He had an exhausted, crumpled look as if he was slowly deflating.

"Well then, is everything okay?" Johnny asked

unable to stand the tension any longer. "Does it look like we're in business?"

"I've gone over all the numbers and you easily have the capacity and the capability to satisfy our requirements. We had no idea that your consumer electrical goods department was actually the smaller part of your business. We knew you dealt in components, but not on such a large scale. Your business is actually bigger and, by the look of things, more efficiently run and competitive than Frankel's. I'll have to discuss the potential deal with Carlo of course, but so far everything is looking good. Theo here certainly knows his stuff. He runs a tight shop."

"As you know we've been dealing with Frankel's for years, but Victor had a stroke two years ago and has had to step down from the business," Carlo said. "I'm afraid his son, Danny just can't cut it. Since he's taken over we've been let down a few times. Obviously Phil and I will want to talk about this, but we should have an answer for you in a couple of days."

Johnny exhaled his bated breath. He felt a rush of adrenalin course through his veins. Bloody hell, he thought, he's done it. He's actually pulled this off, but as grateful as he felt to his friend, all he could think about at that moment was fucking Theo's wife.

***

The Lexus glided silently along, its sophisticated suspension ironing out any flaws in the road's surface. Caitlin didn't speak she was lost in her own thoughts. From time to time she found herself grinning with the thrill of being in such an expensive vehicle. She imagined other drivers seeing them and being envious, wondering how a young couple could afford such luxury. Maybe they would think that she and Colin were famous, a footballer and his wife perhaps.

Colin too, was distracted. What have I done, he thought? I've stolen from my employer. He felt sick to his stomach. He hadn't as much as taken sweets from the newsagent's as a child even though his friends had urged him to do so. If anybody found out what he'd done he'd be fired immediately and no one would ever employ him in a position of trust again. Worse still, he'd jeopardised Caitlin's position too. She worked in the legal professional. She was studying to be a paralegal for Christ's sake.

"Are you all right, Colin? You're frowning," Caitlin's words cut through his thoughts.

"Yes, fine Darling. I'm just concentrating," he lied. "This is a very big vehicle and I'm not used to these roads."

"If you're tired we can go back. Going for a drive in this fab car is enough of a treat for me. We don't need to travel all the way to the coast."

Colin felt a wave of sickness swell in his stomach. Mr. Rigby trusted him. He gave him this job when work was hard to find and look how he'd repaid him.

"We're nearly there now," he said trying to concentrate on what Caitlin was saying. "Don't worry about a thing. In a few minutes time we'll be tucking into dessert. I'll feel better when I have something to eat. The sugar boost will do the trick. The rain's stopped so we'll be able to stroll along the front and take in the sea air before we drive back."

"One day I'll buy you a car like this. You work so hard and you put up with my mum and dad without ever complaining. You deserve the best of everything. Who knows, we might be on our way to riches already. I bought a lottery ticket today, just a lucky dip, but it had both our birthday numbers on it and the date of our wedding, so it might be a sign, I could have the winning ticket. We might win millions."

Colin smiled wryly. At this precise moment, I've more chance of going to jail than of winning anything in the lottery, he thought.

By the time Colin arrived back at the restaurant to collect the Rigby's he had a banging headache. Stealing the blu-rays was the worst idea he'd ever had and now he was stuck with them. It had seemed like such a simple plan, however the reality of his situation was anything but simple. He had no idea how to get rid of them. Who could he sell them to without risking being caught? More than anything he wanted to take them back to the warehouse, but how could he? What would he say to Eddie?

A knock on the car window startled Colin. He hadn't noticed Mr. Rigby was standing beside the car and he leapt out to open the passenger door.

"Sorry, Sir," he muttered. "I was distracted there."

"Don't worry, Colin. I know it's been a long day for you, but we'll soon be home now. I hope your wife will forgive me for keeping you out so late."

"About that, Sir, I hope you don't mind, but I swung round to our house earlier, picked up Caitlin and took her for a drive. I had my phone switched on all the time in case you called so I didn't think you'd mind. I'd like to pay for the petrol," he added fishing into his pocket for his wallet.

"Put your money away, Colin. Of course I don't mind."

Johnny climbed into the car beside Bee and soon they were on their way. When they reached their home he handed Colin a twenty pound note.

"A wee bonus for helping me out tonight," he said. "Take your wife to the pictures or something."

"But, Sir," Colin protested. "You're already paying me overtime."

"I value your work Colin, you never let me down. Get off home now. It's getting really late."

Colin took the money, but felt terrible about it. He'd betrayed Johnny's trust. This is how Judas must have felt, he thought.

TEN DAYS BEFORE

CHAPTER 6

Elizabeth Black tapped her daughter gently on the shoulder and signed to her that it was time to leave. She was in a hurry to get home as she wanted to once again go over the plans for the charity picnic event which was now less than two weeks away. Chrissie pulled a face and held up her open hand, "Five minutes more, please," she mouthed silently. "We've nearly finished."

"Please, Elizabeth," her friend Becky begged. "This email is going to all the local shops asking them to donate tombola prizes for the charity picnic. We've spent ages getting the addresses and we've nearly finished our letter. It's a real tear jerker. They won't be able to resist. If they don't give us stuff they'll look like cruel, heartless losers."

"I thought the idea was to ask them to donate out of the goodness of their hearts, not because they're too frightened not to, Eva," Becky's mother said.

Both girls grinned in response.

"Okay, five minutes more, then we have to go. If I don't do my work there won't be a picnic," Elizabeth said, automatically signing the words to her daughter even though she could lip read accurately.

Chrissie and Becky high fived each other then returned to concentrating on the screen in front of them.

"Why don't I make us a cup of tea? You know their five minutes will become ten at least," Eva said, smiling to her friend.

"Thanks, it's been a busy day, I can certainly use one. For some reason the phone didn't seem to stop ringing today and I couldn't get anything finished. Mr. Rigby's negotiating some deal at the moment and it's creating a lot of extra work. Although I can't complain, he's been very generous in choosing to sponsor my suggested charity this year. He's donating a shed load of money and he said he'll give me some time off to prepare for the picnic."

"His wife's really nice," Eva replied. "She's just started going to my yoga class. I've met her a few times now. She's really funny when she talks about her husband, but she clearly adores him."

"Yes, Johnny and Bee Rigby were childhood sweethearts and I'm sure he loves her very much, it's just a shame he has a roving eye."

"Oh, I love a bit of juicy gossip, tell me more."

"Sorry to disappoint you, but I've no more to tell. I shouldn't have said anything. It's just office chit-chat. You know what it's like when girls get together."

Eva placed a cup of tea in front of her friend. "Tell me more about the charity then. So far, I know it's a children's home and it's the fiftieth anniversary of when it was started, but that's all I know. What's your connection to it?"

"My brother Neil was adopted. Mum and Dad took him from the home when he was ten. He'd been there for about eighteen months. His biological parents were killed and he had nobody who could look after him so he was sent to the Goodheart Home for Boys. After Mum had me she couldn't have any more children and they really wanted another child so I wouldn't grow up as an only one. They chose Neil. I was seven and all of a sudden I had this older brother who I adored. He's a wonderful brother and I love him very much. That's why I wanted to do something for the charity."

"So is it still a home for orphaned boys?"

"No, now it's for boys and girls, but it only houses ten to sixteen year olds. Mr. Goodheart is still in charge even though he's in his seventies and when I checked, the original caretaker was still working there as well."

"How does Neil feel about you raising money for the place? Is he fundraising too?"

"Actually that's rather a sore point. I thought he'd be delighted, but he's not happy about it at all. In fact, he doesn't want anything to do with it. I think maybe he's embarrassed about being a former child of the home. I didn't mention anything to him before I went in with all guns blazing. Now I just want to get on with things and do a good job with the charity picnic. Then I'll never mention it again."

"Well I think what you're doing is great. Everyone is looking forward to it. It's rare these days to be able to have a full day of old-fashioned, family fun and entertainment. Becky's even managed to talk Angus into entering the father's fancy dress race. He's dressing up as a pink rabbit. He's picked up one of those onesies that teenagers are wearing. He looks hilarious. It's not very often we get to socialise as a family what with Angus's job taking him away so often."

Elizabeth had been smiling but now looked as if she might cry. "Neil says he's not going to the picnic. He won't even talk about it and he's forbidden his wife and son from going too. I just don't understand what's got into him. He's normally so laid back."

"Well something has obviously touched a nerve," Eva said. "Perhaps you should just leave well alone. Maybe there's something in his past he doesn't want to relive. Could something have happened to him at the home? Maybe he was bullied or maybe he was very traumatised by the loss of his parents and talking about the place rekindles bad memories."

"I never thought about that. Of course he must still have memories of his birth parents. He was eight when they died. How stupid I've been. I meant well, but I've presumed too much. I just hope he'll forgive me when all this is over."

"Don't beat yourself up about it. You're doing a good thing. I'm sure when it's over everything will go back to normal with your brother. In the meantime we'll all enjoy the day and the Home will receive a boost of cash."

Elizabeth glanced at her watch. "Oh my goodness, look at the time, we really must go now. I'd better get Chrissie. Thank you for the tea and the chat. I feel much better now I've unburdened myself. You should charge by the hour," she added smiling.

"It's okay, I'm a child psychologist not a psychiatrist, my advice to you is free. Just so long as you remember on the day not to tell anyone that the daft looking pink rabbit is my husband," Eva added laughing.

"I promise," Elizabeth replied. "And by the way, my boyfriend will be wearing a purple tutu and fairly wings, so you've nothing to be embarrassed about."

"Boyfriend? I didn't know you had a boyfriend. Perhaps we should just have another cup of tea," Eva said reaching for the kettle.

CHAPTER 7

Eva and Elizabeth had been friends for eight years, but they'd become so close it felt as if they'd always known each other. Reaching the stage in their friendship where each family felt comfortable dropping in to visit the other without a pre-arranged appointment or invitation.

The two women first met at the school gates as they chatted while waiting for their respective daughters. Elizabeth had been particularly nervous, worried how Chrissie, who'd been profoundly deaf since birth, would cope in a mainstream school. Eva, a child psychologist, endeavoured to reassure her without sounding too formal. The friendship blossomed, beginning when their girls emerged from the school together holding hands. Each was grasping a painting.

"Chrissie can't hear. Nothing, not a single word, but she knows what I'm saying when she sees me speaking. It's amazing, she's magic," Becky said excitedly.

"Becky is my very best friend," Chrissie mouthed as she signed to her mother. "I've made a painting of her. See, she has orange hair and blue eyes."

"I told you there was nothing to worry about," Eva said laughing. "Children have no barriers."

"I always worry. I know it's stupid. Chrissie's so bright and she lip reads accurately. I don't know how she does it. If only she had speech, but she refuses to try. She mouths the words as she signs, but won't make a sound."

"I take it she can form sounds, she's not mute."

"Oh, yes, and when she's angry or frustrated she howls with rage, but she doesn't want to speak. She's to see a child psychologist next month at the school, so perhaps we'll get to the bottom of it then."

"I guess we'll get to know each other rather well then," Eva replied. "I'm the child psychologist who Chrissie will be seeing. I only work part-time hours but I'm assigned to this school. I suspect I'll find nothing much wrong with her. She lip reads and signs so expertly she simply has no need for sound. The effort of trying to form sounds would probably slow down her communication. She's still very young and obviously very bright, I'm sure she'll progress normally. Oh, and don't worry, I can sign and Becky's learning to as well."

From that first day the girls became inseparable friends and so did Elizabeth and Eva. With Eva's husband Angus travelling with his job and Elizabeth's husband William choosing to be distant as he pursued other women, they found themselves spending a lot of time together.

Three years ago Eva helped her friend get through her divorce, the dying throws of which were acrimonious. Eva had never liked William. He was sly and unreliable. He never seemed able to look her in the eye when he spoke to her, as if he was hiding something, which of course, he was.

Chrissie had been distraught about the break up, full of anger and grief. She didn't get to spend much time with her father, his choice not hers, but she adored him. She blamed Elizabeth for chasing him away and for a while it caused a rift between them. In the end it was Becky who told Chrissie about William's new girlfriend, she'd overheard their mums talking, and although still dreadfully upset, Chrissie stopped blaming Elizabeth for her pain.

***

Eva and Becky were anxiously waiting for Angus to come home, each straining to hear every time a car drove along the street, hoping it would stop at their gate.

"Is Dad really staying home for a whole month?" Becky asked. "Are you absolutely sure?"

"Absolutely. A whole month."

"And he won't have to work over the holidays? He's going to the picnic in Presley Park with us and he won't have to arrive late or leave early?"

"I promise, Darling, he's not going to travel for a whole month and he's got two weeks holiday from work too. You'll soon be sick of the sight of him. He'll want to hang around all the time and he'll feed you his home-made pancakes and make you play board games with him. He'll even want to go shopping with you and Chrissie and take you both to the cinema and ice skating. How boring will that be?" Eva said laughing.

"Terribly boring, I just don't know how I'll cope having such an attentive, hands-on dad," Becky replied getting the joke and clearly delighted by the prospect of spending so much time with Angus.

Eva missed Angus when he was away. He'd been in the same job for years and it afforded them a good living, but it was tiring for them both. However, they'd been clever and over the years they'd used the surplus money from their earnings to buy residential properties, which they then rented out. The venture was very successful and they were now able to plan for an easier future. During the holidays Angus had an appointment to meet with the owner of a local company who was desperate to employ him. He really fancied the work and, with the extra income from their letting business, Angus was now in a position to consider the drop in salary it would mean. Both he and Eva were thrilled at the prospect of finally having a more normal lifestyle. They hadn't mentioned anything to Becky yet as they didn't want to raise her hopes in case it came to nothing, but they were excited about telling her.

CHAPTER 8

"For God's sake Dolores, get a move on. I'm half an hour late for my kid already and we've a ten minute drive to get there. She'll think we're not coming. Elizabeth will love this. She'll be filling Chrissie's head with more poison about me."

"I'm coming, William. I'm just fixing my lipstick."

"Never mind your damned lipstick. Get your ass down here. You can fix your lipstick in the car."

Dolores sighed and made her way down the stairs. William had become such a boring, old fart recently. It had been fun when they'd first met. It thrilled her having such power over a much older man. William had seemed suave and sophisticated to the teenaged Dolores. Her friends were all envious of the way he splashed his cash around. But now he wanted her to meet his daughter, become part of a family. She didn't want her own kids yet, why on earth would she want to spend time with someone else's?

"You'll like Chrissie," William said. "She's really smart and funny too."

"And she's only six years younger than me, so we'll have a lot in common. Won't we, Pops?" Dolores said cruelly.

"Don't be smart, Babe. It doesn't become you."

William was annoyed. Elizabeth and Chrissie hadn't yet met Dolores. He'd been all set to show off his latest young girlfriend, but now he was worried. Would he look ridiculous with this child at his side, like some sad, old bastard, trying desperately to hold onto his youth? They had nothing in common, except for the sex, of course. He looked at her now, sitting in the passenger seat, fiddling with her make-up, staring at her image in the vanity mirror, and for the first time he saw how young and cheap looking she was. How could he possibly introduce this child as his girlfriend? What on earth was he thinking about? William u-turned the car and parked outside his house.

"Get out Dolly," he said. "I'm sorry. I've made a mistake. This isn't a good time to meet my daughter. It's too soon. She'd only just got used to my previous girlfriend and is probably still getting over our break up. I'll take you with me the next time. Sorry, please get out and go back home. I'm really late."

Dolores didn't say a word when she climbed out of the car, but she slammed the door and strode off, her heels clicking on the pavement.

Thank goodness for that, she thought, saved from the dumb, deaf kid. Now William will have to make it up to me. Probably with a pair of shoes, I think.

***

"I'm sorry, Patrick, we're going to be late. William promised he'd be on time tonight. Something always seems to hold him up. It's so unfair."

Elizabeth stared into the soft green eyes of her

boyfriend, her cheeks burning with a mixture of anger and embarrassment.

"Don't upset yourself, Pet. You know what he's like. We'll be fine because I made the booking for between seven and seven-thirty. I didn't expect him to be on time or even close to it for that matter."

Elizabeth still couldn't quite believe her luck that this strong, handsome, gentle man was her boyfriend. That he'd chosen her as his partner at the singles, dinner club when he could have had his pick from any of the women.

"I don't deserve you," she said.

"You do deserve me," he replied. "Or any of the thousands of men like me. You didn't deserve William. Nobody deserves a selfish, creep like William. That's why all his girlfriends are teenagers. A real woman would see through his shenanigans in an instant."

Chrissie chewed on a piece of her hair, the only outward sign that she was nervous, but inside she was quaking. She really didn't want to meet yet another of her father's teenage girlfriends. The previous two had been stupid and common and they didn't want to share her father any more than she did. Why did he keep choosing bimbos and why did he expect her to spend time with them? She glanced at the clock. Late as usual, she thought. He'll probably blame it on Dolores. What a stupid name. Sounds like some kind of Mexican bar girl from an old movie.

Finally the doorbell rang. Seeing the flashing light to alert her, Chrissie leapt to her feet. "Dad," she mouthed, grinning then ran to answer the door.

"At last," Elizabeth said. "I hope he doesn't disappoint her."

When Chrissie threw open the door, her father smiled and ruffled her hair, "Hello Poppet," he said before striding past her towards the lounge.

Elizabeth was on her feet. She'd wanted to keep William in the hallway but didn't quite make it. Instead, they met awkwardly just inside the lounge door. Patrick jumped up from an armchair.

With Chrissie behind him and therefore unable to see him speak, William said, "Well hello, I'm William, Elizabeth's husband. You must be her latest shag."

Aware that Chrissie had now squeezed past her father into the room, Elizabeth forced a smile onto her lips. "Hi, William, let me introduce you to Patrick Jenkins, he and I are about to go out for dinner. Where's Dolores? I've been dying to meet her. Is she in the car? You should have brought her in."

Patrick covered his lips with his hand as if to stifle a cough so that Chrissie couldn't lip read. "Touche," he said then he smiled benignly and held out his hand to William. "I'm delighted to meet you."

William scowled, "Likewise, I'm sure," he replied. He turned to face Chrissie, "Sorry Poppet, but Dolores couldn't make today. You'll meet her the next time."

Chrissie grinned. Saved, she thought.

"Well, we'd better be going. I've booked us a session, tobogganing at Xscape. I'll have her back by eleven," he said to Elizabeth. "That should give you plenty of time to eat," he added pointedly.

Once the pair had left Patrick took Elizabeth in his arms and said, "He really is a bastard, isn't he?"

"It's the only thing he's good at," she replied.

CHAPTER 9

Carlo Donatelli didn't like confrontations. He preferred leaving delicate situations to Phil McKay. The man was efficient and cold, and if he was affected by being the bearer of bad news, he never showed it. However, because of his long relationship with Victor Frankel, Carlo felt he owed him a personal meeting at the very least. Even though the old man had now stepped down from the business, Carlo felt he deserved that simple courtesy.

"What's the arrangement with Frankel?" he asked Phil.

"We'll go and see Victor at his home in half an hour. We'll leave here in ten minutes. I spoke to him myself so he's expecting us. From there, we'll go straight to Frankel's office for a meeting with his son. Danny doesn't know we're seeing the old man first. Victor didn't want me to say anything. He knows the boy's useless."

"He's hardly a boy, but he is useless. He's frittered away a damn good business. What he's done is criminal and he's let us down so often he could have damaged us too. I'm really sorry for Victor. He's a lovely man. It must be very hard on him."

Carlo and Phil drove to Victor's home in a sombre mood. They were greeted at the door of his impressive mansion by his housekeeper, Aggie.

"Come in, gentlemen, Mr. Frankel's expecting you. I'll be in shortly with tea or would you prefer coffee?"

"Nothing for us, thank you. We won't be staying long," Phil replied and Carlo nodded in agreement.

She walked ahead of them and led them towards a lounge.

"I always feel nervous at these sorts of meetings," Carlo whispered to Phil as they followed. "I feel like such a bastard."

"You feel nervous because you're a nice guy. I feel nothing. It's just another job to me. So don't worry, I guess I'm the bastard," Phil replied.

In the end the meeting took less than fifteen minutes.

"I knew this day was coming," Victor said when they were all seated. "You've been very patient. I'm sorry it's come to this. I gave my son every chance and he's wasted it. Who's getting the contract now? If you want my advice, give it to Rigby's. Johnny Rigby is a real grafter. He won't let you down."

"We haven't decided yet," Carlo replied not wanting to show his hand to the competition even given the circumstances of the meeting. "But he is a contender," he added respectfully.

Carlo and Phil stood to leave. "Take care of yourself, Victor," Carlo said as he shook the older man's hand.

"Thank you for coming," Victor replied. "Good

luck with Danny. I apologise in advance for my son. I should have been harder on him, but you know how it is."

Victor's eyes filled with tears and he turned away embarrassed. "I'm sorry," he muttered. "It's the stroke. It brings all your emotions to the surface."

The housekeeper showed the two men out. Carlo took his handkerchief from his pocket, cleared his throat and blew his nose. "Poor old bugger," he said. "He deserved better."

***

When they arrived at Frankel's they were kept waiting at reception. The minutes ticked by. "Does Mr. Frankel know we've arrived?" Phil asked when they'd been waiting for fifteen minutes without any apology or even being offered a coffee.

"You saw me buzz through," the receptionist replied cheekily. "He's busy with his PA. I'm sure he won't be long. He never is," she added with a smirk.

Carlo was fuming. His face was the colour of boiled lobster and his hands were balled into fists.

"Stay calm," Phil said. "It'll soon be over."

Finally, after another five minutes, Danny and his PA emerged from his office. The girl smoothed her skirt and, as she walked away with swaying hips, she flashed a newly applied, red-lipstick, smile.

"What a gal," Danny said admiringly. "And she takes shorthand too," he added. "Come into my office, Gentleman. Take a seat. Would you like coffee?"

"Half an hour ago, maybe," Phil said and he looked pointedly at the receptionist just as she got to her feet. Then he followed Danny and Carlo into the room and closed the door before she could join them. As they took their seats Phil could see Carlo was still enraged and he placed a warning hand on his arm to stay his temper.

"As you know our current contract with you finishes at the end of the month," Phil began.

"Don't worry too much about the paperwork," Danny interrupted. "We'll keep supplying you as normal until the new contract begins. I trust you to come good."

Carlo exhaled his bated breath. Phil held up a hand to warn him to say nothing before continuing.

"That's the point Mr. Frankel," he said.

"Please, call me Danny, Mr. Frankel's my father," Danny said interrupting again.

Phil was irritated. "There isn't going to be a new contract," he said.

Danny was quiet but only for a moment. "We can't supply you without a contract. It's too big an order for a cash deal. I'm afraid there's only so much can be done under the table. It's a bugger I know, but the taxman always gets his cut one way or another."

Carlo could stand it no longer. "There's not going to be a contract because we no longer wish to do business with you. You've let us down too often. We can't rely on you."

"But you've bought from us for years," Danny spluttered. "You can't just cancel."

"We can and we will," Phil said.

"But what will I do? What will my Dad say?"

"Frankly, I don't give a damn," Carlo replied. "Perhaps if you concentrated more on your business and spent less time with your PA, everyone would be better off."

Danny looked sick and pale. He was deflated and unable to rise from his seat as Phil and Carlo stood and left the room. When they passed the receptionist Phil said, "Your boss isn't feeling well, perhaps you should make him a coffee, if you can find the time in your busy schedule." And with that said they left the building.

CHAPTER 10

EIGHT DAYS BEFORE

It had now been six days since Rigby's meeting with Donatelli and Johnny was pacing the floor. He didn't know what to do with himself. One minute he was storming into Theo's office demanding, "What's he playing at? Why doesn't he place an order?" and the next minute he was whining, "Maybe I fucked up. Maybe we're just not big enough or good enough or well enough established."

"You'll have to keep calm, Johnny," Theo said wisely. "You'll give yourself a heart attack. Donatelli will have to sever his ties with Frankel first then he'll contact us. It's a delicate time for all concerned."

"You're right, you're right, I know you're right, but it's so hard to wait. I'm not functioning. I can't think about anything else. I'll just check with Elizabeth and see if they've accepted the invitation to the charity picnic. If they're coming, surely it would be a good sign."

Johnny strode out of Theo's office and headed for Elizabeth's desk. Oh help, here we go again, she thought when she saw him coming towards her. He was driving her mad. Usually he gave her instructions for the day's work, but this morning he'd been all over the place asking this and that and she couldn't get anything started properly before he changed his mind and gave her something else to do.

"Mr. Rigby," she said as he approached. "What can I do for you now?" she added unable to keep the annoyance from her voice.

"Where are the acceptances for the charity picnic? Not the employee ones, the ones from the dignitaries and invited guests."

Elizabeth reached into her desk drawer and lifted out a bundle of reply cards. "I have them here, but I've also opened a file on the computer so I can see who is coming and who isn't. Is there someone in particular you want me to check?"

"Yes, Carlo and Carlotta Donatelli and Phil and Jean McKay."

"Their invitations were hand delivered only a few days ago. They might not have replied yet," she said.

"Please check the computer anyway, it's very important."

Elizabeth opened the screen. "Nothing on my list yet, but like us, they use Brannigan's mail service and a bundle of mail has just been delivered, give me a couple of minutes to open it and see if anything's there. I'll come through to your office once I've checked."

"I'll wait," Johnny replied and he rested his hands on her desk leaning across it as if ready to pounce. Elizabeth found this action rather alarming and her hands shook as she ripped open the envelopes.

"No, Mr. Rigby, sorry, nothing yet."

"Damn, I was hoping for a reply. How's it going anyway? Are most people coming to the event?"

"Yes, nearly everyone has replied and most are coming. A local DJ has offered his services for free for the children's disco. Everyone has been really generous, but it couldn't have happened without you Mr. Rigby. I'm really very grateful."

"It's a pleasure, Elizabeth. This picnic will do our image no harm and you're doing all the work. I should be thanking you. Sorry, but I've been really stressed recently. It's this deal with Delectra. You know how important it is and we still can't mention anything outside of these four walls."

"Before you go, Sir, let me just check my emails. Just in case something's come in this morning. You never know," she added smiling. "Maybe they prefer email to snail mail."

Johnny leaned across the desk once again.

"Oh, here we are," Elizabeth said, "Something from Mr. McKay."

"Where? Let me read it," Johnny said, coming round the desk and practically shoving her out of the way.

"Here it is," she said, and pointing to the screen, she read, "Thank you for your kind invitation. We'd like to donate two hundred pounds to the charity. Four people will attend on the day."

"Who will attend? Which four people?"

"It doesn't say, Sir. Just four people, no names. Do you want me to telephone them and ask?"

Johnny sighed, "No thanks, Elizabeth. You'd

better not." He looked miserable.

"Surely if you've invited four specific people then they'll be the four who are coming. They wouldn't just substitute strangers when it was a handwritten, personal invitation."

Johnny's face brightened, "You're absolutely right, I'm being too pessimistic. They're coming. Everything is fine. They're coming."

Johnny left Elizabeth and he was in a happier mood when he strode back into Theo's office. "It's in the bag, my friend," he said. "The contract is in the bag."

CHAPTER 11

When Elizabeth called her brother, his wife Jenny answered the phone.

"I'm sorry," she said. "Neil's not available at the moment. I'll let him know you rang."

Her voice sounded strained. Elizabeth got on well with her sister-in-law, in fact, they were quite good friends and often got together for shopping trips or evenings out. Elizabeth knew by her response that Neil was there. Jenny had said 'not available' rather than not in. He was home but refusing to talk to her. This had been the third time she'd rung and she'd yet to receive a call back.

"I'm sorry you can't make it to the picnic," she persisted. "I think the children especially, are going to have a great time."

"Yes, I'm sorry too, but you know what it's like. Neil has other plans for us."

"That's the thing, Jenny. I don't know what it's like. Neil hasn't spoken to me."

There was an awkward silence. "I'm sorry Elizabeth, but I've got to go. I'll let him know you called again. Bye now."

"Bye," Elizabeth replied reluctantly.

The line went dead so Elizabeth hung up.

"You really must speak to your sister," Jenny

said to Neil. "I don't know what's happened between you two, but I'm not lying for you again."

Neil didn't respond, he left the room and made his way to the garden. He needed air. He needed to breathe in fresh air and calm down. His body was tight as a spring. He was full of anger. It boiled inside him and threatened at any moment to explode. He had no idea why he felt this way. Why after all these years the very thought of the Goodheart home unnerved him. As a child he was weak and full of despair, but as an adult he was desperately angry all of the time and sometimes unable to function. He'd never told a living soul what had happened to him at the home, at the hands of that man, that monster. Pushing the whole sordid episode into a locked box in his mind and throwing away the key. Now, once again, he felt helpless. This time was different though, this time he was losing it and he was scared of what he might do.

Like Elizabeth, Jenny had no idea what caused the change in Neil. He wouldn't talk to her about it either. When she'd suggested he see his doctor, his temper flared and he'd hurled the coffee mug he was holding into the sink, smashing it to pieces, before storming out of the room. Neil was usually so placid, so gentle. This sudden mood change was completely out of character.

***

The Goodheart Home was a substantial mansion built from red-sandstone and surrounded by large gardens. It stood in a leafy suburb adjacent to Presley Park and was by far the largest building in the area. At one time it would have been the estate house and all the surrounding land would have made up its grounds.

Lionel Goodheart, who himself was orphaned as a teenager, inherited the house together with a vast sum of money, from his guardian, a distant cousin, when he was in his twenties. Not a single member of the Goodheart family had lived beyond fifty so Lionel felt very fortunate to have reached the grand age of seventy-three and still be on this earth.

His best friend Stanley Jones had moved into the house with Lionel, and for a few weeks they bummed around doing nothing, unsure how to go forward in life. In the end, it was Stanley who came up with the idea for the boys' home.

"You can be the director because you're good with paperwork and I'll be the caretaker because I'm good at fixing things. We'll raise funds as a charity. It shouldn't be too difficult as we're in the middle of one of the wealthiest areas of the city. We can employ day staff, cooks and cleaners and all the boys will go to school to be educated until aged sixteen. Then we'll help them to find work."

His enthusiasm and energy spurred the project forward and within a few months they opened their doors to the city's waifs and strays. Fifty years on, the home housed fifteen children, but at the beginning, before renovation and current legislation, it was home to more than double that number. In the 1960's there were few rules and regulations so Goodheart and Jones had a free rein. Goodheart loved the position of respect he'd attained and he lorded it over his charges like a king, but Jones' needs were much more basic and sinister. The boys in his care were at his mercy and he showed them little consideration.

Elizabeth's brother Neil had been a quiet, shy boy when he first arrived at the home. He was eight years old, slim and delicate with even, handsome features. To his detriment, Jones thought him to be the most beautiful creature he had ever set eyes upon and because of this Neil suffered cruelly at his hands.

None of the boys at the home complained about the ill treatment, although to differing degrees, they all suffered. There was no point complaining. Nobody would believe the words of vulnerable, damaged children. They were the lowest of the low. They had no voice. Instead they just prayed for rescue, prayed that someone kind would choose them for adoption and Neil was lucky. He was one of the few who were saved.

***

Lionel and Stanley were having tea in their private sitting room.

"I'm thinking about standing down as Director," Lionel said. "I'm thinking about retiring."

"Retiring, but what will you do? Where will you live? What will become of me?"

Lionel laughed, "Stanley, my dear friend, we are old men. It's time to stop working and have some fun while we still can. We're fortunate that we still have our health and money is no problem. We can do whatever we want. Go wherever we please. Would you rather keep working here until you die?"

"I guess not," Stanley replied. "I've always fancied a trip to Phuket, it looks so exotic, or maybe India. With our money we'd be kings in India."

"Sounds good to me. We can give our notice to the charity and make an announcement at the picnic. I'm not so sure about Phuket but I'll happily join you on a trip to India. As for where we'll live, I've seen a 'for sale' sign go up on 'Albany House'. It has four bedrooms, three public rooms and three bathrooms as well as a pool house, a sauna and a granny flat. We could employ a live-in housekeeper. Give her the granny flat. What do you think?"

"I can see you've been thinking about this for a while. When are we booked to view the house?"

Lionel laughed. "You know me too well, old friend. Actually, I've made us an appointment for tomorrow morning."

CHAPTER 12

Theo arrived at his office the next morning and shut his door. He'd had yet another altercation with Mandy about some trivia and he wasn't in the mood to talk to anyone. Usually, the first fifteen minutes or so in the morning were spent chatting with colleagues and coffees being poured before everyone got down to the daily grind, but not this morning. Theo's secretary was to be late in for work because of a dental appointment. His assistant accountant, Tom, was deeply ensconced in a conversation with Johnny and Elizabeth and the two typists were comparing nail polish. Nobody even noticed Theo slip into his room.

As he removed his jacket and draped it over the back of his chair his mobile rang and when he looked at the caller ID he saw it was Mandy. His heart skipped a beat, but he hesitated from answering because he couldn't bear being drawn into yet another argument. Theo had no idea what had changed recently between them, but he couldn't seem to get anything right. What was distracting her and making her irritated and distant was a mystery to him. Some days she was excited, chatty and attentive, but the rest of the time she was bored and their conversation was limited to one word answers or worse, developed into a fight.

He heard the familiar beep, beep beep as a text

message came in and when he read it, it was Mandy reminding him not to be late home as she was going out for the evening and he had to babysit Charlie. He had no idea where she was going or with whom and he was frightened to ask because he wasn't sure he'd be happy with her reply.

Theo switched on his computer screen and scanned his emails. It took a second look before he realised there was one from Phil McKay of Delectra. He opened it with bated breath. It read, 'Theo, lovely to meet you and your charming wife. I'm pleased to tell you we are now in a position to place a sample order. Attached, I've listed our requirements. You'll note this covers monthly deliveries for the next three months at the previously agreed terms. As long as you can meet these orders, in full and on time, I see no reason why we can't firm up a more permanent arrangement in the new year. Please confirm receipt of this email and your agreement to its contents. Best regards, Phil.'

Theo was ecstatic. They'd done it. They'd won the order. He covered his face with his hands and rested his elbows on the desk in front of him. He felt very emotional and it took him a few minutes to compose himself. If Mandy hadn't already made another arrangement he would have called her and suggested they go out for a celebratory dinner, somewhere that Charlie would enjoy as well. Instead he and Charlie would have to celebrate with a carry-out and a movie.

He printed off the email and the order, placed it

in an envelope and walked towards Johnny's office. Wishing to savour the moment he casually handed the envelope to his boss. Light blue touch paper and stand back, he thought. Johnny was rabbiting on about football. As he removed the contents of the envelope and scanned it, suddenly his chit-chat stopped mid-sentence.

"Bloody Hell, Theo! Bloody Hell! It's only a fucking order. We've done it. It's a fucking order," he exclaimed.

Johnny grabbed Theo in a bear hug and kissed him on the forehead. "We've only gone and got a fucking order," he yelled. Johnny ran into the main office holding aloft the printed email. "Everyone, listen up. I have here, in my hot, sweaty hand, an order from Delectra. Elizabeth, send out for champagne and cream cakes," he instructed. "This calls for a celebration."

Amidst all the excitement and back slapping Theo felt sad and lonely. He really wanted to celebrate with Mandy. The trouble was, so did Johnny, and it was Johnny, not Theo, who'd be spending the evening with her.

Once the excitement dissipated Theo realised there were important checks needing to be done in advance of the first consignment. He called Tom into his office.

"On computer it looks as if we have ample stock to cover the first order," he began. "However, there is always the possibility that the numbers on the computer don't actually tie up with what's in the store. Until we do a stock audit we can't account for damaged items, incorrect recording of transactions or indeed theft. We have to be absolutely sure we don't mess up. I'd like you to take an assistant and physically check that each item on this order is accounted for. I want all of Delectra's order to be separated from the rest of the stock in anticipation of the delivery date. Liaise with Eddie, the warehouse manager, but don't leave this job to the warehouse staff. I need you to oversee it, okay?"

"I understand, Boss. Don't worry, if something doesn't add up. I'll find it. It will take a while, but I'll ensure our recording system is accurate and if not, I'll find out why. Nothing will jeopardise this order," he assured emphatically.

"Good man," Theo said. "If we can pull this off effectively, they'll be a Christmas bonus this year. You might be able to treat yourself to that season ticket you've been going on about. As long as your missus doesn't get her hands on the money first," he added with a laugh.

When Tom left his room, Theo tried to call Mandy. Maybe she'd offer to change her arrangement when she heard his news he thought, but the phone rang out until the answer service kicked in. Theo hung up, declining to leave a message.

When the excitement died down, the first thing Johnny did was to call Bee and tell her his news. He apologised for not being available to take her out to celebrate that evening, explaining that he had to work late.

"Marie's having tonight off so we couldn't go out anyway. She's meeting up with some friends who are also au pairs. So we wouldn't have a sitter."

"We'll have a big celebration on Saturday," he promised. "Anything your heart desires, my sweet. Anything, any place, any cost, your choice."

When Johnny ended the call to his wife he immediately telephoned Mandy from his mobile. "Fishnet stockings and black suspenders tonight," he said. "We're celebrating. I've got something I want to give you. Something big," he added lewdly. "Expect to be late home. I've booked us a room at the Central Hotel. The honeymoon suite," he added with a laugh.

Mandy got a thrill every time she thought about the evening ahead. Carefully selecting her sexiest underwear made her positively wet with anticipation. The risk they were taking by meeting in such a well known and prestigious place heightened her excitement. And the thought of having dirty sex with another woman's husband made every nerve in her body tingle with desire.

Poor Theo, she thought, stuck at home with a pizza watching some inane movie with Charlie while she was drinking champagne and fucking his boss. Oh, well, it's his own fault, she was moving up while he was content to mark time.

CHAPTER 13

Colin was washing the company car in the car park in front of the warehouse. A stand pipe was against the wall, still operational from when the previous company, a builders' merchant, had used the space. Eddie was chatting to him as he worked.

"Those blu-rays okay then?" Eddie asked, making small talk.

"Yes, I guess so, no complaints anyway." Colin looked down and polished the side of the car vigorously. He could feel his cheeks burning.

"Just let me know if the boss needs anything else signed out," Eddie offered. "That looks like hot work. Do you want a cold drink? I've got cola in the fridge. Yup, all mod cons in this store," he laughed.

"No thanks, you're all right, Eddie. I'm nearly finished then I've to take the boss into town for an evening meeting."

"Ah, but have you to bring him back again or is he spending the night? Wink, wink, know what I mean."

Colin was about to respond when both he and Eddie saw Tom coming towards them.

"Oh, oh, here comes trouble," Eddie said. "I wonder what he wants. He never stoops so low as to come round here. I usually get prissy little emails full of please and thank you from him."

When Tom approached he nodded at Colin. "Boss asked if you'd pick him up now. He's ready to leave." Then he turned to Eddie. "Can we go into your office please? There's something we need to discuss."

As Colin climbed into the car he called out to the older man. "No rest for the wicked."

Then immediately each of them thought, how true.

***

Mandy arrived at the hotel before Johnny. She wanted to surprise him. Her neighbour Molly came to sit with Charlie so she could leave the house before Theo got home. Charlie didn't mind, he liked Molly. She made great cup cakes and she never arrived empty handed.

The arrangement had been that Mandy should sit in the hotel lobby at eight o'clock and await Johnny's call. He would then tell her which room he was in and she would join him. It was barely seven-thirty. Mandy's idea was that she would pick up the room key and a bottle of champagne and be ready and waiting in the bedroom in all her finery for his arrival, but she hadn't thought her plan through. She had no idea what name he'd booked the room under and she knew he'd be annoyed if she drew attention to their liaison. So Instead she had an uncomfortable wait, constantly looking out of the door of the main entrance, so she could watch for him arriving.

At seven-thirty-five Colin pulled the car into a parking space beside the hotel entranceway just as Mandy popped her head out of the door. Each was surprised to see the other. Johnny's expression on seeing her was of a trapped animal.

"Wasn't that Mrs. Walker?" Colin began and immediately regretted his words, suddenly gauging the situation.

"No, it wasn't," Johnny replied shortly. "I didn't see her and neither did you. Drive me home, Colin. My meeting has been cancelled."

Colin said nothing more, but as he pulled the car away from the hotel, he could see Mandy's dismayed expression in the rear view mirror.

"I'll remember your discretion, Colin," Johnny said. "If ever you need a favour just let me know."

Colin liked his job and he respected his boss. He hated that he'd stolen from him. He didn't know what to do with the blu-rays. He didn't know how to get rid of them. They were still hidden in his father-in-law's garage.

Colin began to think, he began to formulate a lie as they drove along the busy streets of the city centre, something to get him out of the mess. Something his boss would believe. Finally, he blurted, "I've done something stupid, Boss and I didn't know how to tell you."

Johnny's thoughts had been all about his situation, but now Colin had his full attention. Colin concocted a tale of misunderstanding and confusion. He said he'd overheard a discussion about picking up items from the warehouse which were to be donated for the raffle and got the wrong end of the stick. He'd collected the blu-rays and signed for them, thinking that's what was required. However, after he'd collected them he realised he'd got it terribly wrong and the raffle prizes were being delivered directly.

"I panicked, Boss. I didn't want anyone to think I was trying to steal them. I didn't know what to do with them."

"Where are they now? Have you disposed of them?"

"No, of course not, Boss. I knew they weren't mine. I just didn't know how to return them. I didn't want to get Eddie into trouble for handing them out without an official order being placed through the computer. They're at my house, in the garage. I've kept them perfectly safe."

"So let me get this right. You went to the store and asked for stock saying they were prizes for the picnic and Eddie just handed them to you?"

"I had to sign for them, Boss. I wasn't hiding anything. I genuinely thought I was helping out."

"What exactly did you sign? What did the order form look like?"

"Just a sheet of paper itemising the stock, I didn't really read it."

"It sounds to me as if you've been very foolish, Colin, even if your intentions were good. But as you well know, everyone is capable of making a mistake," Johnny said wryly. "I don't want you to say anything about this to anyone. We'll go to your house and collect the blu-rays. You can leave them in the boot of the car. If I hear you've mentioned this to a single person, you'll be dismissed immediately for misconduct. Do I make myself clear?"

"Absolutely, Boss, absolutely. I'll not forget this, Boss. I'm sorry I've been so stupid. I'll never let you down again."

Colin's eyes filled with tears of relief and he swiped at them with the back of his hand, sniffing loudly to stop from sobbing. Johnny too, could have cried. What a fucking awful end to one of the best days of his life. Betrayed and let down by people he trusted and sexually frustrated as well.

***

Mandy was shocked to the core. What on earth should she do now? She began to walk away from the hotel along the busy city centre high street. Her heels were impossibly high and her underwear, although stunningly sexy, was beginning to feel rather uncomfortable. It was designed to titivate then be removed, not for wearing for any length of time while trudging along a busy street. She didn't want to go to a bar, but how could she arrive back home so early? What explanation could she give to Theo? Johnny was going to be livid. His driver had clearly seen her. What a mess. Oh, God, what an awful mess.

Having walked a relatively short distance, just out of sight of the hotel entranceway, Mandy found herself outside a Starbucks coffee house. With little other choice of a place to sit down that wasn't a bar, she entered and ordered a double espresso. She needed a strong hit of caffeine to help her gather her thoughts. Mandy had only managed a sip of the scalding liquid before a man, seated at an adjacent table, leaned across.

"Are you okay," he asked. "You look a bit uncomfortable sitting there on your own."

Mandy was about to reply when he continued.

"These stools aren't really designed for high heels and suspenders and I'm sure they make scanty panties chaff a bit too. I could help you take them off if you'd like," he added leeringly.

The man had removed his wallet and was flicking through twenty pound notes.

Oh my God, Mandy thought, he thinks I'm a prostitute.

"I'm meeting my husband," she stammered. "I'm just killing time. I'm early."

"Dressed like that? Of course you are," he replied. "Better luck next time then, Doll. Your 'husband' is one lucky guy, a rich guy too by the look of those fishnets."

The man stood, gulped down the last dregs of his coffee then licked his lips suggestively at her before leaving. Mandy waited a moment then practically ran out of the shop and immediately hailed a taxi. She had to get home, had to get changed out of these clothes. No wonder that horrible man thought she was a hooker. She was dressed like a whore and she'd been intending to meet a man who wasn't her husband, to have sex in a hotel. Her cheeks were burning with shame. What a stupid fool she'd been, thinking she looked classy and sexy when in fact she looked cheap and sluttish. Is that how Johnny saw her, she wondered?

CHAPTER 14

Emma and Alex Rigby were watching a film on the television when they heard the Lexus pull up. They were on their feet and in the hallway before Johnny could put his key in the door.

"Daddy's home," they called out simultaneously to Bee who was in the kitchen. She stopped what she was doing and she too made her way to greet him.

"Daddy, Daddy," the children cried, launching themselves at him before he could properly get through the door.

"Mummy's making hot chocolate," Alex said excitedly.

"With marshmallows," Emma added.

"Aw, I wanted to tell Daddy about the marshmallows," Alex whined.

"Now, now no bickering," Johnny chided. "Where's Marie?" he asked Bee hoping the au pair would give them some respite so they could talk alone for ten minutes.

"She's having the night off," Bee replied. "Don't you remember I told you? She asked for Friday evening because it's her friend's birthday and they're meeting up with a group in town.

"Oh, yes, you did say, my mind's mince at the moment. It's full of too much information. I think I'll just have to clear my head by tickling small children," Johnny said holding up his hands and gesturing. "Are there any children here who require tickling?" he asked.

Alex and Emma squealed excitedly and took off along the hallway towards the sitting room.

"Run, Alex, run!" Emma exclaimed. "Daddy's turning into the tickle monster."

"Once that pair are in their beds the tickle monster will come and get you," he said to Bee, with a leer.

Bee laughed, "Not the most romantic thing you've ever said to me, but I get your drift. I'd better finish making the hot chocolates then. Just don't get them too hyper or they'll be up all night."

As Johnny ran after his squealing children he thought, 'how stupid I've been, risking all this for a tawdry fling with my best friend's wife. But at least I've been lucky, it's over. I've had a close call and a lucky escape. Sometimes you don't realise what you've got until you risk losing it'.

***

Mandy slipped quietly into the house. She could hear Theo and Charlie in the lounge and, from the sounds emanating from within, they were still watching their movie. Quickly, she ran upstairs to change as she didn't want either of them to see what she was wearing. It took her only a few minutes to throw on her comfy jeans and sweater then she went to the bathroom and removed her make-up before reapplying a light lipstick. She was at the top of the stairs ready to descend when Theo opened the lounge door and called.

"Mandy, is that you? You're early. Is everything okay?"

"Everything's fine, Theo. One of the girls I was meeting couldn't make it and the other girl had a terrible day at work and ended up with a banging headache, so the evening fizzled out. What have you two guys been up to?"

"We had pizza, Mum," Charlie replied happily. "I got five different toppings and Dad bought ice cream from the cafe and popcorn for eating during the film, just like in the cinema. We've been watching James Bond. He's so cool, Mum. There's popcorn left, we couldn't finish it. Do you want some?"

"I've actually only had a coffee. We didn't get round to ordering food so I'd better get something solid to eat first," Mandy replied.

Theo thought Mandy's face looked rather strained. He didn't know what actually went wrong with her evening out, perhaps she fell out with her friend, but he didn't care, she was home now and that was all that mattered.

"Go and relax in the lounge. Have a chat with Charlie while I make you a sandwich and a cup of tea," he offered. "Is ham and lettuce okay? We've got that in the fridge or I could phone for a carry out if you'd like something more substantial?"

Mandy looked into her husband's kind eyes. His face showed fatigue and yet here he was running after her.

"A sandwich would be great, thanks," she replied.

As Theo disappeared into the kitchen Mandy thought about her day. How stupid she'd been, risking everything she had. How had she and Theo got to this stage? When they were younger they couldn't get enough of each other. What had changed? He was thoughtful and good natured, a wonderful father, who only wanted to love her and take care of her and their son. Their love life had been exciting before, perhaps it could be that way again. She'd been so busy trying to win over Johnny, trying to have a quick fix of excitement that she'd let her relationship slip. But Johnny Rigby would never love her like Theo loved her. She could see now that he'd been using her. When Johnny looked at her he saw what the man in the coffee shop had seen, a tarted up piece of skirt that could be bought for a few drinks. She'd been kidding herself by thinking he'd ever leave his family for her. He didn't love her and he never would.

"Do you want mustard on your sandwich, to spice it up a bit?" Theo called to her from the kitchen.

"No mustard, thanks," she replied. "A plain sandwich is fine. I don't like things too hot."

***

Once the children were in bed Bee and Johnny sat at the kitchen table. He hadn't eaten for hours and he was beginning to feel faint from hunger. Not long after he'd arrived home he opened a bottle of rich, red wine to let it breathe. Now he was looking for something to accompany it.

"What can I make you to eat?" Bee asked.

"If you don't mind, I'll just have some of that

brie with baguette and perhaps a piece of tarte tatin."

"My, my, you're becoming very French. It must be Marie's influence. Next year, when she leaves to go to uni, let's get an au pair from Italy and perhaps she'll make us spaghetti carbonara and some of that wonderful lemon tart we both like."

"I guess we were very lucky getting an au pair who could cook."

"Yes," Bee replied. "One of the girls I meet at yoga told me her au pair set fire to her kitchen. Speaking about yoga, I met a friend of your secretary's at the gym."

"What, a friend of Elizabeth's?"

"Yes. Did you know Elizabeth has a brother called Neil?"

"I knew she had a brother but I didn't know his name or anything about him. Why do you ask? Is it relevant to anything?"

"Well, apparently Neil has stopped communicating with Elizabeth because of the charity picnic. Eva Logan, that's my friend, thinks it has something to do with an experience he had at the children's home. She's really interesting. She works as a child psychologist."

"I'm sorry for Elizabeth, of course I am, she's worked very hard for this event, but her relationship with her brother is her business. Eva can't be much of a friend if she's discussing her with all and sundry."

"I'm hardly all and sundry," Bee replied indignantly. "She only mentioned it when I told her my husband was the boss of Rigby's. The boss who has just won the contract of his life," she added smiling and trying to lighten the mood.

"I still can hardly believe it," Johnny replied, grinning. "We're moving into the super league now and I couldn't have done it without your support. You're some gal, Bee Rigby. With you by my side I can achieve anything. I love you so much."

Bee had heard these words of praise before and she knew Johnny was telling the truth. She knew he loved her above everything else. So why, she wondered, did he look at other women and why from time to time did he stray?

***

Both Theo and Mandy felt rather fatigued so they decided to retire for the night not long after Charlie went to bed. Theo decided to have a warm soak in the bath to ease his tired muscles. Mandy, had showered earlier in the day to prepare for her evening with Johnny and her skin felt soft and was perfumed. Entering the bedroom she reached under her pillow for her pyjamas then changed her mind. Throwing them into the laundry basket, she instead donned a slinky, satin nightgown. Mandy liked the feel of it on her skin as she slid between the cool sheets. Then she turned off the harsh, overhead lighting and switched on the bedside lamps. The room took on a pleasing glow.

When Theo climbed into bed beside her he was surprised when Mandy moved towards to him. She rested her head on his chest, "I'm so proud of you for winning the contract with Delectra," she said. "I know that it's Johnny's company, but you're the brains when it comes to the figures. He couldn't have done it without you."

Mandy raised her head and gently kissed her husband on the lips. Theo felt a stirring in his loins, but was unsure what to do. He didn't want to take anything for granted and risk another fight. It had been months since they'd made love.

Mandy reached out and ran her hand gently, down the length of Theo's torso. There could be no mistaking her intentions now. He turned to her and began to make love to her with patience and tenderness. She responded with passion. Both were relieved to be bridging the rift that had developed between them.

When their passion was spent, Mandy lay in Theo's arms and gradually drifted off to sleep. This has been a perfect day, Theo thought and, smiling to himself, he gently kissed Mandy's head inhaling the sweet fragrance from her hair.

CHAPTER 15

Eddie Maxwell was arrogant and stupid, two of the faults his wife screamed at him as her reason for leaving him, when she exited their home for the last time, finally slamming the door on their marriage. He'd been smug and contemptuous when Tom advised him about the stock audit he intended to carry out. Two more flaws his wife had hated about him. According to her, the list was endless.

"It's alright by me," Eddie said to Tom. "But I suggest you bring someone who can operate a fork lift to help you because most of the stuff you'll want to see is on the upper level. I can't allow anyone who isn't licenced near the fork lift or the cherry picker. It's more than my job's worth," he added with a chuckle. Eddie had never been too worried about rules in the past.

"Supercilious number cruncher," Eddie muttered after Tom had left him, "Namby-pamby prick, thinks he can teach me my job. I'd like to see him check those boxes on the upper level. Oh, yes, I'd love to see that."

Eddie knew that some of the cartons held empty boxes, but they looked the part. They were all sealed and they all had the correct number of boxes inside. If some of the goods were found to be missing, then perhaps it could have happened at the manufacturer's packing house. Nobody would be able to prove that Eddie had removed the goods, besides the anomalies would be miniscule on the scale of things.

His real coup, however, and what they'd never discover, was any errors in his paperwork. Every item removed from the lower level had a completed order form to cover it. Eddie knew the system was flawed as it didn't properly correlate the 'on-paper' only orders, delivered to small retailers, with the computer raised orders dispatched to larger consumers. And, there was no correlation between items which went out one month with 'on-paper' only order forms, to the date these items were actually entered on the computer. So particularly at month ends, the stock might look short only to seem over by the beginning of the next month.

Tom detested Eddie and he was desperate to catch him out. The only reason Eddie held the position of warehouse manager was because he'd been a friend of Johnny Rigby's father. He neither looked the look nor talked the talk for a manager of a department representing a business the size of Rigby's.

***

When Johnny woke the next morning, he showered and dressed before reaching for his mobile. Although it was the weekend and the offices were mostly closed, he needed to speak to Theo about what he'd discovered from Colin. He wanted Theo to brief his assistant and ask him to conduct the audit immediately. There was no time to waste. They had to be sure that all the stock for Delectra was in place well before the first delivery date. If Colin could remove stock without it being noticed, then what else might be missing? One thing was sure though, Eddie had to know what was going on. Johnny made himself a mug of instant coffee as he dialled Theo's number. On the eighth ring, just as he was about to hang up, the call was answered.

"Bloody Hell, Johnny, do you know what time it is? It's Saturday for Christ's sake."

Johnny glanced at the clock on the kitchen wall. The time was 7.45am.

"Oh, Jesus, Theo, I'm sorry. My mind's buzzing. I didn't realise it was so early. I'm really sorry, Mate. I hope I haven't woken up the whole house."

"Mandy and I had rather a late night, if you know what I mean," Theo answered, pleased with himself. "She'll be grumpy if she has to get out of bed too early and I'll be grumpy too, if she gets up before I do," he added crudely.

Theo was feeling on top of the world and he wanted his friend to share in the banter.

"I know exactly what you mean, Mate. Bee and I had quite a session too. I guess women are turned on by powerful men and you don't get much more powerful than winning the Delectra contract. Just as well, because you're an ugly, old bastard. If you weren't in a position of power, you'd never get a fuck." Johnny started to laugh at his own joke.

"Cheeky sod," Theo replied, laughing too. "What do you want anyway? It must be important for you to leave the marital bed and phone me at this ungodly hour."

"I have reason to believe that Eddie Maxwell is ripping off the warehouse. I'm pretty sure he's stealing stock and has been for years."

"Eddie Maxwell, the store manager? But he's been with us forever. He was your dad's best friend. You look after him very well. Why would he steal from you? Are you absolutely sure?"

"Ninety-nine per cent positive."

"Bloody hell, you must be gutted."

"I am, but I need to prove what I think is going on. I need the paperwork to back it up and that's where Colin Anderson comes in."

"Colin the driver? What's he got to do with anything?"

"Eddie gave out stock purely on Colin's say so. He fabricated paperwork to back it up. It was for ten blu-ray recorders. I might be wrong, and I sincerely hope I am, but I'd be willing to bet the paperwork will be for more than ten items. Worse still, this fraud might be the tip of a very large iceberg."

"Oh fuck, I guess Tom and I will be working today after all. I'll go and phone him right away and tell him the bad news. I'll pull a team together. We'd better go in with all guns blazing before Eddie has a chance to cover anything up. I'm sorry, Mate. This wasn't the sort of news we needed after all our success. It's a real bubble buster. We should be celebrating today not finding out the people we trusted have fucked us over."

CHAPTER 16

Change made Stanley Jones nervous. The thought of no longer living at the Goodheart Home and no longer holding the position of head caretaker, made him very unsettled. He was used to having power over people, especially the boys who resided there. The staff loved Stanley. They thought he was a great man, a benevolent benefactor. He was always obliging and helpful, always smiling and cheerful.

He selected his victims with great care, always choosing troubled boys, often ones who'd been abused by a parent in the past. Boys who expected nothing better or were too weak and frightened to complain. He wasn't physically abusive. He never raised his hands to any of his charges, quite the reverse, in fact. He'd shower the chosen boys with gifts, or treat them to outings before taking them to his bed, and afterwards, when they cried with pain and humiliation, he'd hold them in his arms and comfort them.

He didn't believe his actions were abusive. He loved the boys he bedded. Even long after they left the home, Stanley would offer them his support, both financially and emotionally and they, in turn, let him make love to them. Stanley didn't know what he'd do if he had to leave the Goodheart Home. He liked boys, the younger the better and the home afforded him an endless supply of fresh meat.

Lionel Goodheart knew all about Stanley's dalliances, but he chose to ignore them. After all, it didn't really hurt anyone. In third world countries it was quite normal for men to lie down with boys. Nobody complained, nobody reported him, so there wasn't a problem. However, with the recent hullabaloo over the Jimmy Saville case, the time was right for them to move on before someone did open their mouth or tried to blackmail them. It was always about money and he had no intention of giving any of his away, especially not to some undeserving little bastard who he'd helped.

***

The weather had been hot and stifling for days and it had now become heavy and oppressive, so it came as no surprise to Elizabeth when the sky blackened, hailing an impending thunder storm. She was expecting Eva and Becky to arrive at any moment to have lunch with her and Chrissie. They'd been intending to visit the park after lunch and physically walk through the layout for the charity event, but that wasn't a good idea in a storm. The one place they didn't want to find themselves was walking under trees when there was lightning. So Instead, Elizabeth gathered all the paperwork and plans and spread them out on the dining room table for their perusal after their meal.

Everything was ready for lunch and had been laid out in the kitchen. The meal was combined, rather than cooked, as it was too hot to eat anything other than salad and cold cuts. With Chrissie's enthusiastic help, Elizabeth had baked a strawberry flan for dessert. The kitchen table was set. She had sparkling apple juice for the girls and a bottle of Chardonnay for the adults, chilling in the fridge.

Eva had been particularly delighted with the lunch invitation as her husband Angus was attending a lads' golf day with his friends. Not that they'd be playing much golf in a storm, although she guessed it had always been their intention to spend more time at the nineteenth hole than any other. This lads' day out was held once a year and Angus always came home roaring drunk after it with tales of holes-in-one and winning scores. He usually arrived home around nine then passed out in his favourite armchair in front of the television. She didn't have to worry about him though, as the lads always hired a mini bus for the occasion and the driver was very well rewarded for putting up with their drunken revelry.

Elizabeth wanted the opportunity of speaking to Eva about Neil. She realised Eva treated children not adults, but having pondered about the dramatic change in his behaviour, she wondered if perhaps it was something in Neil's childhood which had triggered the change. His wife Jenny had rung Elizabeth only yesterday because she too was worried and didn't know what to do about him.

"I'm actually rather scared for him, Elizabeth," she'd confided. "His behaviour is quite bizarre. He's been getting up through the night and sleeping behind the sofa. When I find him there in the morning and wake him up, he doesn't remember getting out of bed. Then there are his mood swings. One minute he's stomping around the house losing his temper over the least little thing, and the next minute, I think he might burst into tears. He won't go to his doctor. I can't even discuss it with him. It's something to do with the children's home. I'm sure it is. Joe is very frightened by his dad's behaviour and now he's begun to act up too. I don't think I can cope much longer."

Elizabeth too felt that the picnic was the catalyst which had set off Neil's erratic behaviour, but she didn't know what to do about it either. Her only hope was Eva. Surely she'd have some suggestions that could help him. One thing was certain however, they couldn't go on this way.

***

Neil sat in his car outside the Goodheart Children's Home and watched as people came and went. He had no idea why he'd gone there. It was the last place he wanted to be. He sat there for hours as the rain battered the windscreen. So far the monster hadn't appeared, but Neil knew eventually he would return. When he'd telephoned earlier, a woman, probably a housekeeper, had said he was out for the afternoon, but Neil could try again after five-thirty. She'd asked his name so she could leave the monster a note and Neil made one up. He didn't want to warn him he was coming.

Six-fifteen and still no sign of him, Neil was stiff from sitting in the one position for so long, but he didn't want to get out of the car. He didn't want to feel exposed. He'd wait until six-thirty then he'd leave, just fifteen more minutes. The time came and went. At six-forty he turned the key in the ignition. Then he saw him. Even with his head bowed against the rain, Neil recognised him instantly. He sat with the engine running watching the monster approach. The rain streamed down the windscreen.

Neil began to shake. His body was bathed in sweat. During the hours he'd sat there outside the gates, he'd planned over and over in his mind, the exact words he wanted to say to the monster. Now all he could do was tremble and cry like a baby. He was cowed and terrified. He was eight years old again.

CHAPTER 17

Carlotta heard the honk of a car horn and reached for her umbrella.

"That's Justin at the door, Carlo. He's just parked outside. Enjoy the grand prix on the telly. I wish I was watching it with you. Singapore today isn't it?" she called.

Carlo came out of the den to embrace his wife. He marvelled, that even with her hair scraped back in a band and no make-up on her face, she looked stunning.

"What will you be wearing at the shoot today?" he inquired. "Are you filming in a studio?"

"Evening wear, in a city centre hotel, mock catwalk show, hence this," she replied, grabbing the handle of a wheeled suitcase. "Five pairs of my size eights. I was asked to bring black or silver shoes because it's for a Christmas catalogue. The whole shoot is to be practically monochrome. Typical Justin, arty stuff, lots of funny angles."

"A bit like his parking, then," Carlo replied glancing out of the window. "Why is it women and gay men can't park? Look how he's left that car, it's abandoned not parked."

Carlo opened the front door to see his wife out just as large spots of rain began to bounce off the ground.

"Hurry up, Dahling," Justin called to her as he struggled to haul open the door of the people carrier to let Carlotta climb in. "Oh help, my hair. Don't you just hate rain?" he added.

Justin was skinny, waif-like, his hair looked like a Mister Whippy ice-cream cone, pure white and ending in a pointed quiff. Carlo chuckled watching him struggle with the door. Even though Justin reminded him of a cartoon character, he knew this strange young man was a genius behind the lens of a camera and was Carlotta's photographer of choice.

There were two other girls in the car with Justin, and Carlotta had worked with both of them before. Erika was extremely thin, skeletal with white skin so fine it almost seemed transparent. Her hair too, was nearly white as were her brows and lashes. Photographers loved Erika. She was a blank canvas ready to be filled in any way they chose. The other girl, Titania, Tanny for short, had a milk-bottle white complexion and a profusion of fiery red hair. With Carlotta's ebony skin and long limbs thrown into the mix, the three made a striking picture.

"The catwalk and lighting are all set up," Justin began as they drove off. "Ken and Barbie have been at the venue working since dawn."

Ken and Barbie were Justin's technical assistants and were, in fact, both men. Although looking at the androgynous pair it was hard to tell.

"I've hired eight extras from rent-a-crowd. They'll all be dressed in black and I've got these great, pill-box style hats with lacy veils so we won't see their faces clearly in the photos. They'll simply be a crowd of faceless onlookers. The whole tableau will be mostly black and white except for some dark green holly and, of course, Tanny's red hair. I've only got the hairdresser and make-up girl for part of the day as they're going on to another shoot, so we'll have to try and get it right first time. Oh, and the bad news is, there's only one dresser so you might have to help each other a bit."

"So what time are we aiming to finish?" Carlotta asked.

"Probably around six o'clock if all goes to plan." Justin replied. "Why, have you got another job to go to?"

"No, not really, Carlo's friend is coming round to watch the grand prix then his wife is joining us later. We're planning to have dinner together. I thought I might cook something, that's all," she replied.

"Cook? You? After a full day's filming?" Justin said. "Do yourself and your friends a favour and order a carry-out. I've never heard such rubbish. Remember I've tasted your cooking before."

***

Phil arrived just before lunch carrying some plastic food boxes and a six pack of beer.

"Jean sent this," he explained. "Some stuff to eat while we watch the grand prix. She said we've not to spend the whole day just drinking beer and you've not to smoke too much."

"Even when our wives aren't with us, they manage to nag," Carlo replied laughing. "Carlotta said exactly the same thing to me before she left for work."

"I do hope Button wins today," Phil said. "He's in pole position, but everyone seems to fancy Vettel to take it."

"Yeah," Carlo replied. "I'm afraid the smart money is on Vettel. He's having a great year."

"Have you heard anything from Danny Frankel?" Phil asked. "I thought he might call one of us and try to win back the order."

"No, not a word, but knowing Danny, he's probably drowning his sorrows or blowing his mind with cocaine. I feel really sorry for Victor. He's such a good guy, old school, honest and hard working. I'm so glad my boys turned out okay. I was very tough on them when they were growing up. I even made them do chores for their pocket money."

"You obviously got it right, Carlo. Maybe if Danny hadn't been handed everything on a plate, he would have appreciated it more."

"Right my friend, enough talk about work. Let's go into the den and get ready for the day ahead. You switch on the telly, open the food Jean sent and I'll get us plates and some more beer."

Phil did as he was told and Carlo waddled off to the kitchen for more supplies. Soon they were seated in the den munching on sausage rolls, mini pizzas and salad sticks with dip.

"This is a feast," Carlo said approvingly.

"And the beer's pretty good too," Phil added. "I prefer your Czech beer to my Belgian, but both will hit the spot nicely."

"We're going to smell like a brewery by the time the girls get here, but never mind. Where is Jean anyway? What's she up to this afternoon?"

"She's playing bridge with the three witches, her old friends from college."

"That sounds rather dull."

"The bridge is dull, but I've heard the conversation is lethal," Phil replied. "You know what it's like when a group of women get together, they'll be ripping everything and everyone to shreds."

Carlo chuckled, "I don't think I'll ever understand women."

"We don't need to. Just be glad they're not here to criticise us," Phil added, handing Carlo another beer.

***

The photo shoot ended exactly on schedule as everything went to plan. All concerned were delighted, particularly Justin.

"Well done, children," he enthused. "There won't be any bonuses paid of course, anything extra goes straight into my pocket, but you'll have my sincere thanks and undying gratitude."

Although Justin had collected the models in the morning that was for his benefit not theirs, to ensure they were on time for the shoot. Now each of them had to make their own way home. Carlotta was first in line at the hotel reception desk to call for a cab and was climbing into her taxi before anyone else arrived. Her bag was haphazardly packed, but she didn't care, she just wanted to get home and have a shower before Jean arrived.

When she got back, she found Carlo and Phil still in the den with the remains of their food and empty beer bottles in front of them, strewn across the large, square, opium table.

"I'm just going to have a shower," she said. "What's the plan for dinner?"

"No plans yet," Carlo replied, "But Phil and I quite fancy a curry."

"Isn't it strange how you always fancy a curry in the height of summer yet crave ice-cream when it's freezing cold outside? Okay," she conceded, "If Jean wants a curry too, then please order an assortment of starters and mains from the 'Tandoori House'. What time do you think she'll get here?"

No sooner had Phil glanced at his watch than the doorbell rang. "I guess that answers your question," he said. "That's probably her now."

"You get the door, Carlo. I'll be down in a few minutes," Carlotta said and she disappeared upstairs to freshen up.

Before very long they were all seated in the dining room tucking into a variety of dishes from the Indian restaurant. Inevitably the discussion turned to the contract with Rigby's.

"I'm just surprised that you feel we have to go to this charity picnic event," Carlotta said. "None of us have young children, so I don't know what we'll do there. I don't think there'll be much to interest us."

"Oh, I don't know, hot dogs and candy floss sounds good to me," Phil said.

"Me too," quipped Carlo.

"You two are like a pair of overgrown children sometimes," Jean said. She and Phil exchanged pointed looks then grinned at each other.

"What?" Carlotta asked, "What's going on with you two?"

"We didn't want to say anything until it was confirmed," Phil began.

"We've only just found out, Jean added. "We've been approved by Social Services. We've been approved to adopt."

"Fantastic news," Carlo said jumping to his feet and slapping Phil on the back.

"We're so happy for you," Carlotta agreed, hugging Jean enthusiastically.

"We're no longer young, but it seems that we're not too old to adopt an older child. Lots of couples in their forties adopt older children. "The best news is that there are children already in the system. As an example, we've been told about two siblings, a boy of four and a girl of six."

"They're with a foster family at the moment," Phil added. "We know the whole process will take time and we might not be considered a suitable match for these particular children. We've also been advised that there could be some behavioural problems given their circumstances, but we're sure we'll cope. We've wanted a family for so long."

"Well then, that puts a whole new perspective on the picnic in the park," Carlo said. "I'll expect to see you taking part in some of the events, Phil. You'll need to get into practice, and don't worry, I'll take my camera and make sure I record every last detail," he laughed. "I can't wait to see you cavorting about. I don't think I've ever seen you in shorts in all the years I've known you."

"Neither have I," added Jean, grinning happily. "But I guess there's a first time for everything."

CHAPTER 18

FIVE DAYS BEFORE

Danny Frankel liked to drink and he loved to party. After his meeting with Carlo and Phil he did both, in abundance. Danny had lots of drinking buddies. He was well known at all the swanky bars and nightclubs, frequenting only the most exclusive. Money was no object and it ran through his fingers like water down a drain. His accountant had warned him on numerous occasions to slow down his spending and be more frugal, but Danny ignored him. As long as there was cash in the bank account or his credit was good, he didn't have a problem. But now he'd been told there was no more cash in the company bank account, there was barely enough to pay the wages at the end of the month and once news got out about Delectra, his credit wouldn't be good either. There was nothing else for it he'd have to speak to his father.

Victor's bank account was robust and healthy, positively bursting at the seams. Danny knew he had more than enough stashed away to last him until he died. The silly old sod never spent a penny, never had any fun, he never partied, even when he was young. Danny had been putting off the meeting, putting off the inevitable berating he'd receive, but now he'd run out of time.

He took a bottle of whisky from his desk drawer and poured a large measure of the golden nectar into his coffee mug then gulped it down hungrily. Dutch courage was required. There was a knock on his office door and he could make out the shape of his secretary through the opaque glass panel. Quickly, he returned the bottle of scotch to the drawer, sat up straight and ran his fingers through his hair.

"Enter," he called.

Catherine opened the door and strode in. She had been Victor's secretary before Danny had taken over the business and she was a solid woman in her late fifties. A no-nonsense spinster who took pride in everything she did. She fully understood Danny's shortcomings and reported his misdemeanours to Victor on a regular basis. Although no longer involved in any legal or financial sense, Victor watched sadly from the sidelines. He couldn't bear the thought of his name being tarnished.

"Yes Catherine, what can I do for you?" Danny asked when she came in.

Catherine was clutching a sheaf of paperwork. "It's the August delivery from China. It should have arrived last week but it didn't. I telephoned their office and they said they've put a stop on the order because of a problem with the previous month's payment. I've checked all the paperwork and we instructed the payment through the bank so I telephoned the bank to find out what's happened and they've referred me back to you. Have you any idea what's going on? Most of this month's requirement for Delectra is in that consignment."

Danny felt sick to his stomach. He'd hoped the Chinese would send the order assuming the non-payment was just a glitch. They'd been supplying Frankels for over ten years. He couldn't understand why they were so jumpy about one month's delay in payment.

"Leave it with me and I'll sort it out," he replied unconvincingly.

"When I checked back, our payments to them have been getting progressively later each month. I have the paperwork here for two more of our overseas suppliers and neither of them has been paid for last month's delivery either. Something is seriously wrong, Mr. Frankel. I think you might have to make an appointment with the bank manager."

Danny felt his heart drop to his boots. 'Christ,' he thought, 'I'm in the shit now. The word is obviously out about our late payments. Soon everyone will be withholding their orders.'

"I said I'll sort it, Catherine," Danny answered sharply. "Leave the paperwork on my desk and shut the door when you leave."

Catherine hovered for a moment unsure whether to challenge him further. Her mouth was dry and she swallowed hard trying to dislodge the lump that had formed in her throat. She was scared, she felt helpless, suddenly realising that the loony had taken over the asylum and there was likely to be no way out.

Danny poured himself another shot of whisky,

then another and another until the bottle was empty. He was drunk enough to be slurring his words before he left his office to visit his father. He saluted a worried looking Catherine as he passed by her desk stumbling over her wastepaper bin on his way. Then he popped into the local Crown Inn for just one more, before hailing a cab. Immediately he was out of the office, Catherine rang Victor. His housekeeper handed him the phone.

"Hello Catherine," he began, "How nice of you to call. Is everything okay?"

Catherine had intended to stay calm, she didn't want to upset Victor, but the words tumbled out between sobs and she couldn't help it.

"It's the company, Sir. I think we're going under. There's no money in the bank and suppliers haven't been paid. This month's wages have already been transferred, but after that we're cleaned out. Mr. Frankel junior is on his way to see you and I'm afraid he's rather intoxicated."

"Oh, Catherine, I'm so sorry. I knew the boy was useless, but I thought he'd learn as he went along. I see now that was a pipe dream."

"What will happen to all the employees, Sir? Many of us have worked for Frankels for years, but compared to some, like Tony in packing, I'm a relative newcomer. Will everyone lose their jobs?"

"If what you're telling me is correct then I'm afraid that will be the case. I'm so sorry Catherine, that boy of mine has done nothing but break my heart."

When the conversation ended Victor slumped in

his chair. He'd been worried this day would come. Well, he thought to himself, Danny has had all he's ever going to get from me. Any money left after I've gone is tied up in a trust fund to sponsor a student award scheme at the university. He's frittered away his chance, but I'll not allow him to spoil someone else's.

As Victor awaited the arrival of his son he began to get angry. All my life I've worked like a slave building my business, he thought, and now it's been lost, drained away on drink and parties. We were the forerunner in our field, for years we've been the top company, we've even won awards for God's sake. How could he lose it all in such a short time?

Weary and leaning heavily on his cane, Victor walked towards the door of the lounge. He summoned Aggie and filled her in on what Catherine had told him.

"I'm so sorry, Victor," she said saddened by the look of fatigue on his face. Victor was more than her employer, he was her friend. "What can I do to help you?"

"Nothing, there's nothing anyone can do. Danny only visits me when he wants something and once he discovers I'm not going to bail him out, I'll probably never hear from him again. I'm just glad his mother isn't alive to witness this day."

"So you think he's only coming here to ask you for money?"

"I'm sure of it."

"He's going to get angry, Victor, when he realises you're not going to help him. Do you think we should let him in? He might lose his temper and hurt you. You're not really fit for a physical confrontation."

"I'm not scared of that little shit. I'm twice the man he'll ever be, even in this state," he replied, spittle forming on his lips.

Aggie wasn't so sure. In her years prior to being employed by Victor she'd worked in many bars. She knew how violent drunks could become when they didn't get their own way, so when she left the room she telephoned her son who did gardening work in the district, to see if he was working nearby.

"Just give me five minutes, Mum, and I'll be with you. I'm only round the corner. I'm just finishing off Mrs. Reece's garden. You can make me a cup of tea. Working in this heat, I'll be ready for one."

"Thanks, Son," Aggie replied.

She was relieved. Her boy Billy was six feet six and built like a wrestler. Victor wouldn't even know he was in the house because he'd come round to the back door, but just in case things kicked off, she'd feel better knowing he was around.

***

Aggie and Billy were sitting at the kitchen table when the doorbell rang.

"That'll be him now," she said rising.

"Leave the kitchen door open, Mum, so I can hear what's going on."

"I'll leave the lounge door open too if I can or else I'll stand outside and call you if I need you."

With trepidation, she made her way to the front door. Victor stood in the hallway.

"Why don't you sit in the lounge, Victor, and

I'll bring him through," Aggie offered.

"No," he said determinedly, "This is as far as he gets. We'll talk here."

With pursed lips Aggie opened the door and Danny practically fell through it.

"Agatha, dear Aggie," he began. "Don't you think that sounds like a problem page? Dear Aggie, my son is in need of much money. Should I help him?" Danny laughed and stumbled towards his father. He stank of alcohol. The smell seemed to be seeping out through his pores. "Hi Pop. You've probably heard already from Catherine. She never could keep a secret. She should be called a blabbery not a secretary," he slurred, laughing at his own joke. "I've fucked up, Pop, and only you can help. Actually, only your money can help. It's lucky you've got shed loads."

Victor was seething, he was white with rage. His face was contorted and he was finding it hard to speak. He grasped his cane so hard his arm was shaking. Danny tried to focus.

"You don't look so hot, Pop. You're not having another stroke, are you?" Danny said this with no hint of concern in his voice.

Aggie stepped towards Victor and grasped his elbow.

"What's this?" Danny said, laughing. "Is there something going on I don't know about? It's hardly original, the housekeeper and the wealthy employer. Is Aggie going to be my new Mummy? Surely not."

"Get out of my house, you disgust me," Victor's voice was little more than a whisper.

What was that, Pop?"

"I said get out of my house," he repeated his voice rising. "You'll not get a penny more from me even after I'm dead. I've tied up everything in trusts. Now get out of my house and don't contact me again."

Unsteady, but with a look of determination on his face, Victor turned towards the lounge.

"Danny is just leaving," he said to Aggie. "Please show him out and if you have any trouble, please summon Billy from the kitchen to help you."

"You knew," she said. "I'm sorry, Victor."

"I saw him come through the gate," he replied. "Don't be sorry. I'm grateful to you both."

With that, Billy came out of the kitchen, took Danny by the arm and half carried, half dragged him to the front door before throwing him onto the ground in the garden.

"You heard your Dad," he said. "Don't come back."

CHAPTER 19

When Eddie arrived to open up his office at eight o'clock in the morning, he was surprised to find the door already unlocked and even more surprised to find Tom sitting at his desk and two security guards leaning on the counter drinking coffee.

"Aye, aye, what's all this then? Wives locked you out? I don't usually see the office boys in work so early."

Tom immediately stood up. The slight of being referred to as an office boy wasn't lost on him. "Are those your keys, Eddie?" he asked pointing to the key ring Eddie had thrown down onto his desk.

"Keys for here, yes, not my house keys, why, what do you want with them? Is there a problem with one of the locks?"

"We've been carrying out an audit over the weekend and I'm afraid we've discovered some anomalies," Tom began.

Eddie visibly paled but he didn't flinch. "What do you mean anomalies? I keep a tight ship here. All my paperwork is in order."

"I'm sorry Eddie," Tom said. "But I'm not prepared to discuss this at the moment while our investigation is still being carried out. Tom reached forward and picked up Eddie's keys. "I'd like you to now gather up any personal belonging you have here and remove them from your office. Then I want you to leave the premises. You will be paid while the audit continues, but I don't want you to come into work. If you're in a union then you should let them know what's happening and I suggest you might want to speak to a lawyer. The union can help you with that if you don't have one."

"This is ridiculous," Eddie spluttered. "Give me back my keys. I'm not leaving here until Johnny Rigby tells me to leave. I was his father's best friend you know. I've got years of history with this company. You have no right to speak to me that way." A line of perspiration beaded on Eddie's forehead and a tic developed under his left eye making him look as if he was winking. He rubbed at his eye with his balled fist.

Tom showed no emotion. "Either you gather up your stuff and leave here of your own accord or these gentlemen will escort you off the premises," he said nodding towards the two security men.

Eddie glared at Tom then he walked round to the back of the reception counter and wrenched open a drawer in the desk. The strength of his action caused the drawer to slide right out, spilling its contents. "Damn," he said as he scrabbled about on the floor to retrieve his belongings. He stuffed several items into a plastic carrier bag.

"You'll be sorry when you go through my paperwork and it shows that nothing's wrong. Then I'll get a lawyer and I'll sue Rigby's for slander. You'd better watch your back you fucking little shite. This is all your doing. I blame you personally." Eddie shouted into Tom's face spraying his cheek with spittle. With each word he made a stabbing motion with his forefinger towards Tom's chest. "Watch your back office boy. You've taken on the wrong man."

Tom was frozen with fear. Eddie had madness in his eyes, like a trapped, crazed dog. The two security guards stepped forward and stood on either side of Eddie, each placing a restraining hand on him. He angrily wrenched his arms from their grip.

"Don't touch me," he yelled. "I'm leaving."

As he neared the door he kicked it open with force, cracking the lower panel of safety glass. One of the guards reached out his hand to grab him but Tom stopped him. "Let him go," he said. "His goose is cooked and he knows it."

***

Colin went into work on Monday feeling relieved that the truth was out and grateful that Johnny Rigby had forgiven him. He dreaded being confronted by Eddie knowing that he'd betrayed him, but all he cared about at this point of time was self preservation. Besides, he reasoned, if Eddie's done nothing wrong then he's got nothing to worry about.

When he turned up at the main reception to collect his work schedule for the day, he was asked to take a seat.

"One of the big bosses wants a word," the receptionist told him.

"Mr. Rigby?" Colin enquired.

"No, Mr. Walker, he asked me to phone him

when you came in."

"Lucky I'm on time then," Colin joked.

He sat down on one of the comfortable armchairs, rested his elbows on his knees, held his chin in his cupped hands and waited for Theo to appear. He didn't have long to wait though because a few minutes later he was asked to go through to a small interview room. Theo was already seated inside.

"Hello, Colin, come in and be seated, please."

Colin felt a wave of apprehension rush over him. There were papers on the desk in front of the boss and on the top he could see what looked like the order for the blu-rays. This meeting was beginning to feel rather formal. It was most unusual for Mr. Walker to have any contact with Colin. In fact, Colin hardly ever saw the man.

"Would you like a coffee?" Theo offered.

"N no thanks, I've just had breakfast," Colin stammered and he fidgeted in his seat like a naughty schoolboy facing a headmaster.

"I'm getting some sent in anyway. So you can change your mind later if you want."

Silence resumed while Theo read through a couple of papers.

Colin's right leg began to tremble uncontrollably and he pressed his hand on it in an attempt to stop his foot from knocking on the floor. There was a rap at the door and a woman entered carrying a tray with a pot of coffee, a plate of biscuits, two china cups and saucers and a matching milk jug and sugar bowl. The china was covered in a pattern of full blown roses and looked rather twee for the circumstances. Both men watched in silence as she placed the tray on the desk then left and closed the door.

"Now then, about this order form," Theo began, pushing a piece of paper towards Colin. "Tell me about it."

Colin felt as if all the air had been sucked out of the room. He pulled at his collar trying to ease the pressure. He felt his throat constrict as he struggled with nerves.

Noting the younger man's discomfort, Theo poured himself a black coffee and waited, patiently sipping the scalding liquid.

"I told Mr. Rigby what happened. It was a misunderstanding and he knows all about it. He said everything was okay." The words came streaming out, with undisguised panic in Colin's voice.

"Is this the order form Eddie Maxwell asked you to sign?" Theo asked pushing a paper towards him.

Colin peered at the order. It looked similar and it carried the familiar mark he'd scrawled as his signature, but the amount was wrong. This order was for twenty, not ten, blu-rays.

"It's the form I signed, but the amount isn't right. This order's for twenty but I only signed for ten."

"That's what Mr. Rigby thought," Theo said. "I've taken the liberty of having a statement typed up to that effect. I want you to read it carefully and, if you think it's correct, I'd like you to sign it. I'll ask one of the girls to come in and witness your signature, but don't worry she won't see the content of the statement. This is purely for our records only."

"Should I get a union rep to assist me?" Colin asked nervously.

"Have you done anything wrong?" Theo replied. "If you read the statement it says there was a misunderstanding. You're only being asked to confirm that the number of blu-rays was changed from ten to twenty after you signed for them."

Colin scanned the document. It's Eddie they're after not me, he thought and he felt instant relief. The stupid bastard's tried to rip off another ten machines on the back of mine. Well, Hell mend him, it's not my fault he got caught.

"Okay, Mr Walker," he said, "Where do you want me to sign?"

Before Colin left the confines of the interview room he was given strict instructions not to contact Eddie.

"Mr. Maxwell is on leave at the moment so he won't be on the premises," Theo advised.

"Don't worry Mr. Walker," Colin replied. "I understand what he's done and the statement I've just signed. I won't be going anywhere near Eddie Maxwell. He's got a foul temper and I don't want to find myself on the receiving end of it," he added.

CHAPTER 20

Chrissie Black and Becky Logan were popular girls in school even before being involved with the charity picnic. But handing out personalised invitations to their classmates entitling the bearer to a free ice cream at the event, courtesy of the local cafe, made them even more popular. Since she'd joined the high school all Chrissie's classmates had learned to sign and she loved being able to communicate with them freely. Their teacher had asked the two friends to prepare a presentation to advise everyone at school about the picnic and tell them about the facilities which would be available in the park on the day, as well as the various events and competitions. The girls had planned their presentation with Becky speaking and Chrissie signing. They mentioned the bouncy castle, the treasure hunt, the fathers' fancy dress race, which had diplomatically been named the men's fancy dress race because many of the participants weren't actually the fathers of the children they represented. For instance, Chrissie was content for her mum's boyfriend, Patrick to take part. She liked Patrick and he was kind to her, he was certainly more reliable than William, but he wasn't her dad.

William had yet to tell her whether or not he would be coming to the picnic. Chrissie had resigned herself that even if he did attend, the dreaded Dolores might accompany him. She would forgive him anything if only he'd be there for her. More than anything she wanted to enjoy the event with her dad.

By the time the girls had finished their delivery, the children were thrilled by what lay ahead. As they filed out of the gym hall where the assembly had been held, each was given a flyer to take home giving useful information about the event. Everything from parking and toilet facilities to games and food suppliers was mentioned together with the list of fabulous prizes for the competitions. The buzz of excitement reached a crescendo as everyone discussed their plans.

"Is the prize for the egg and spoon race really going to be a digital video camera?" Becky asked Chrissie.

"Yes," her friend replied, "And there are two of them, one for the adult's race and one for the children's. There are going to be heats throughout the day with the final races being held at two-thirty. Mum says the cameras are top of the range. Rigby's has supplied the prizes for each of the competitions and they're all great."

"What's the prize for the decorated cake competition because I'm going to enter that?"

"The latest Samsung tablet. It's bright red and it looks really cool. You're a real artist when it comes to cakes. I hope you win."

Little, if any work was done that morning because neither teachers nor pupils could think of anything but the picnic. There were few social events in the year which included the whole community and everyone was looking forward to this one. They all thought it would be a perfect day, one for the photograph albums. Even the weather forecast was favourable.

***

Elizabeth was angry with William. He hadn't yet said whether or not he was coming to the picnic and Chrissie kept asking her if he'd called. How could he treat her so shabbily? She was his only child and he was always saying how much she meant to him. With Neil adamantly refusing to come, William was Chrissie's only hope of having a male relative attend the event.

When lunchtime came around Elizabeth went outside to the car park to call him on her mobile and read him the riot act. Her hands were shaking with anger as she dialled his number then waited for her call to be answered.

"Yes, Elizabeth, what do you want?" William's voice sounded strained.

Elizabeth berated him, "How can you leave her hanging on like this? You're her father and you see little enough of her as it is."

William sighed, "Has it ever occurred to you that I might be having problems of my own? It's always been the same, Elizabeth. Everything is always about you and what you're doing. No wonder Neil's not going to the thing, he's probably sick of hearing you blowing your own trumpet yet again," he added cruelly.

Elizabeth was stung. Tears welled up in her eyes. Could William be right? Was she the reason Neil wanted nothing to do with the picnic?

There was a moment of silence before William spoke again.

"Tell Chrissie I'll be there. Of course I'll come. I'm not sure what time I'll get there, but I'll find her when I arrive."

The phone went dead. Elizabeth took out her handkerchief, dabbed at her eyes and blew her nose. Even after all this time, William still had the ability to make her cry.

***

William wanted to hurt someone because he was hurting. It just so happened, that Elizabeth's timing was perfect and she was the one on the receiving end of his frustration. When he'd returned from his evening out with Chrissie the night before, Dolores was at their home and she was drunk. Worse still, she was still partying with her friends, another teenage girl and two boys who weren't much older.

"Oh, oh, your dad's home," one of the boys said when William entered the lounge.

Delores was sprawled across the sofa with her head on the lap of the other boy. She didn't even bother to sit up when she saw William.

"Hey, old man, do you want a beer?" the boy offered pointing to the cans on the coffee table.

The other girl laughed nervously. "That's not her dad," she said. "It's her boyfriend."

The boy on the sofa looked shocked. He pushed

Delores off him and stood up. "We'd better be going," he said. "Sorry man, she told us this was her place. She didn't say anything about a boyfriend. He grabbed his friend by the arm. "Come on, we're leaving. Are you coming with us?" he asked the other girl. She hesitated for a moment then grabbed her bag and followed them.

"Call me," she said to Delores as she left, making a gesture with her hand mimicking holding a phone to her ear.

It was the wake-up call William needed. What a fool he'd been. How could he ever have thought this would work? Within the hour he'd packed up Delores' belongings and packed her off in a taxi, handing the driver a twenty pound note and telling him to head for the city centre.

"But where will I go?" she wailed through the open window as the cab pulled away.

And with the unforgettable line from 'Gone with the Wind' he'd replied, "Frankly, my Dear, I don't give a damn."

CHAPTER 21

THREE DAYS BEFORE

The Goodheart Home and its adjacent park stood almost at the centre of the community. A mere five minutes drive away was Albany House, situated at the end of a wide avenue, in an upmarket, suburban cul-de-sac, but to Stanley Jones it might as well have been on a different planet. He and Lionel Goodheart had already had a first viewing of the house and his friend had fallen in love with the majestic mansion. Stanley couldn't fault the building either. It was spacious and stunningly presented with every luxury he could imagine. In fact, all that was missing was access to partners for Stanley's nocturnal pleasures, but as far as he was concerned, that was the most important part of his life. He didn't care that there was a covered swimming pool and a sauna or indeed, a home cinema room. He wanted to remain where he was and be surrounded by children, so he could have his pick from the endless supply of vulnerable young boys. Without sex, power and control, he was nothing and his life might as well be over.

"Do you want to drive or will I?" Lionel's words cut through his chain of thought.

"You drive, I'm feeling a bit tired today,"

Stanley replied.

"It's probably excitement. I couldn't believe it when I saw the house for the first time. I never dreamt we'd be able to retire to such luxury and at such a fair price."

Stanley didn't reply. He was lost in his own thoughts. Lionel headed for Albany Avenue, which was a long street of two and three bedroom, semi-detached houses culminating in the imposing Albany House. It was a quiet location favoured by middle-class families in the catchment area for the best schools.

Neil and his family lived about halfway along Albany Avenue in a three bedroom house. They weren't particularly high earners but they economised on other things so they could afford to live there and give Joe access to the school. When Neil and Jenny married, their first home was a lower priced apartment in Thirsk Road, round the corner from where they now lived. It was a bit too close to the Goodheart home for comfort, as far as Neil was concerned, but the location was very handy for both of them to be able to get to work.

"Are you sure you've got all your stuff?" Neil asked Joe as they made their way along the avenue. "We don't want to get to the scout hall and find you've left something behind."

"Yeah, Dad, I've got everything. I only really need my swimming badges to prove I can swim the required distance and my life saving certificate."

"I'm so proud of you son. You're clever and you're good at sport. Good man."

"I wish we could go to Aunty Elizabeth's picnic, Dad," Joe replied. "There will be lots of games and competitions. Everyone is going. I'm the only one who won't be there."

"Yes, I know, Son, but I've already got plans for the weekend and I don't think I can change them."

"Even if you can't go, Dad, couldn't Mum take me? I know it wouldn't be the same without you," he added quickly.

"My plans are for us all, as a family," Neil replied flatly. "Get a move on slow coach," he said looking at his watch. "We're going to be late."

They had almost reached the point where Clevedon Road, the street which housed the scout hall, bisected Albany Avenue, when Lionel's car came into view. Neil's jaw dropped with shock. He could see Stanley's smiling visage. The car was only feet away from him. Stanley's eyes were fixed on Joe who was wearing his cub-scout uniform. He saluted the boy as the car rolled slowly past.

"Who is that man, Dad? Do you know him? I think he knows us, he just gave me the cub salute."

Neil struggled to reply then he snapped, "We don't know him. He's a stranger. That's how children get stolen away. They get into stranger's cars thinking it's someone they know. Keep away from people like him. They're dangerous."

Joe was taken aback by Neil's outburst. He knew all about stranger danger, he wasn't a little kid. He was about to protest until he saw the look on his father's face then he thought better of it. He didn't understand what had happened to his dad, but something had changed and Joe was worried about him and rather frightened. They walked the short distance to the scout hall in silence. Neil deposited his son, started to leave then turned.

"I'll be waiting at the door when you come out. Don't walk home with anyone else. I'll be there," he instructed.

A few of the parents were standing chatting, but Neil didn't stop. He gave them a nod then walked quickly away.

The last time Neil had seen Stanley Jones he'd felt sheer terror and had been reduced to a quivering wreck, but the sight of that monster saluting Joe changed something in him. How dare he? How dare he make contact with my son? This ends now, he resolved. I've got to stop that monster before he harms anyone else.

When Stanley saw the little boy looking so cute in his cub outfit with his skinny legs poking out of his shorts, his heart skipped a beat. Maybe a street full of family homes wasn't such a bad move after all. There must be plenty of children living here and surely one or two of them would like to spend time with a kindly grandfather figure. Especially if he had a private swimming pool and offered to buy them expensive gifts.

CHAPTER 22

When Phil McKay arrived home from work, Jean came into the garden as he parked in the driveway. She stood wringing her hands nervously as he climbed out of the BMW.

"Are you okay, Jean? "Is something wrong?"

"Quite the contrary, something is very, very, right. Come into the house and I'll tell you."

When they entered the lounge Phil placed his briefcase on the floor and removed his jacket throwing it over the back of an armchair. Jean lifted a slim cardboard file off the coffee table.

"Helen, our social worker came round today and she gave me this," Jean said, holding the file out in front of her. "It's a profile of a child. A little boy called Peter. He's six years old," Jean's voice caught in her throat and a sob escaped her lips. "He could become our son, Phil. He's available for adoption and his profile suits ours. We've to take a few days to consider everything then meet Helen at her office on Monday morning."

Phil sank down onto the sofa. He was stunned by the news.

"What about the two siblings she told us about before? What's happened to them?"

"I don't know, Helen just said that on reflection

they weren't a suitable match for us. I didn't ask her any more about it because it didn't seem appropriate. Besides, she gave me the file on Peter. Open the file, look at his photograph, he's a lovely little boy."

Phil opened the folder and began to read. "Parents dead, lived with maternal grandmother for nearly five years, no other living relatives. Grandmother has advanced MS, now in a care home. Poor little mite, he hasn't been very lucky, has he?"

"He's with a foster family at the moment, but they are only supposed to have him for a short term and he's already been there for longer than intended. The grandmother has signed all the papers to allow him to be adopted. Apart from being a bit short sighted, he doesn't seem to have any disabilities or behavioural problems," Jean added. "He even looks like you, Phil. Anyone seeing the two of you together would assume he was your natural son."

Phil stared again at the photograph of Peter, Jean's right, he thought, the boy did resemble him. Jean sat down on the sofa beside Phil and he immediately placed his arm round her shoulder and gave her a hug. She raised her face and looked into his eyes. Phil kissed her full on the lips and grinned.

"It's really happening, we're going to be a family," Jean said and once again a sob escaped from her lips.

"Don't upset yourself, Darling. This is great news."

"I'm crying because I'm so happy, you idiot," she wailed and punched him lightly on the arm. "When should we tell people?"

"Well, I think we should wait at least until we see Helen on Monday. Then if all goes well, we can phone my sister and your Mum."

"My Mum is going to be so excited. She thought she was never going to be a granny," Jean said.

I'd like to tell Carlo and Carlotta, of course," Phil added. They're our best friends and if all goes well, I'm going to want quite a lot of time away from the office."

"Of course we'll tell them," Jean agreed. "They're like family to us."

"I still can't quite believe this is happening. I just hope the boy likes us, what if he doesn't want us to be his parents?"

"What's not to like?" Jean replied. "We'll be great parents. Of course he'll like us. I'm sure he'll love us, and, just to be sure, we'll buy him a dog. Even if he thinks we're naff, no kid can resist a dog," she joked.

***

As was their custom, Carlo and Carlotta chatted about their day as they dined together. The subject inevitably came round to Phil and Jean. With their news about being accepted as prospective, adoptive parents, recently the conversation always seemed to turn to them.

"You know their lives will change completely," Carlo said.

"So will ours," Carlotta added. "They're our best friends and at the moment our whole social life revolves around them."

"Not our whole social life, mia cara, but I agree, a lot of it does. I remember when my boys were young. They came everywhere with us. We couldn't do anything spontaneously, everything had to be planned to the last detail."

"That's what I mean, at the moment we can call them at the drop of a hat to go out for dinner or to the cinema. Then there are the weekends away, and what about Christmas? We're booked to fly to New York. We'll have to cancel if they get given a child or children."

"I've raised my kids," Carlo said. "I'd hate to go through all that again. They need so much attention. You could probably cope with it because you're young, but I certainly wouldn't want to."

The minute the words were out of his mouth Carlo regretted them.

"I'm sorry, mia cara," he said. "I'm a selfish man. In all the years we've been together I've never once asked you how you felt about having kids. I just assumed you were content with our life the way it is."

"I am more than content, my darling, I'm perfectly happy. I love you and I love my life. I don't want to have children. I'm close to your sons and they are enough for me and I must say, I'm glad they're adults and we're free to enjoy ourselves without being burdened by youngsters. I'm just really sad that our lives will change when Phil and Jean become parents."

They sat in silence for a few moments each contemplating their changing situation.

"It will feel like bereavement," Carlo finally said. "It will be as if the old Phil and Jean passed away and were replaced by a family."

"I suppose we'll just have to work at courting new friends," Carlotta replied, but even as she said the words she felt unsettled by the prospect.

CHAPTER 23

Danny Frankel opened his eyes and tried to focus. His surroundings seemed familiar, but everything looked askew. His head was sore, he was too warm and his right arm lay numbly across his belly. He couldn't move the arm. It felt floppy like a dead fish. He massaged it with his left hand, squeezing and rubbing it until gradually the sensation of pins and needles painfully brought it back to life. Danny stared, his eyes searching, as familiar things came into view, trying to judge where he was. Slowly it dawned on him that he was lying on the floor of his dressing room, half in and half out of his walk-in closet, with one leg resting on the shoe rack. His clothes, still on their hangers, were strewn around him and his head lay at an uncomfortable, awkward angle, propped up on his gym bag.

Danny leaned on one elbow and straightened out his body, stretching his limbs and groaning. He had a vague memory of going into the closet to look for more booze, but everything after that became a blur. Stiffly he rose to his feet and stretched again. He felt sick and staggered towards his bathroom almost kicking over his plastic, wastepaper bin, which was full of empty bottles and cans and soaked with urine.

Danny attempted to remove his clothes, but was

still partially dressed in his shirt and underpants when he turned on the shower and climbed in. Standing under the cool jets, as he gradually emerged from his alcohol fuelled haze, his first thought was, 'God I need a drink'.

Danny remembered going to a bar after the confrontation with his father. He remembered drinking with people he knew, but at this precise time, he couldn't say what day it was or whether it was morning, noon or night. One thing he was sure of though, when his credit cards stopped working and his cash ran out, so did his friends.

'God', he thought, 'I must have a drink'. Danny searched his house for something, anything alcoholic, but found only empties. Then he searched the pockets of his jackets and trousers for forgotten fivers or tenners, but found none. The only cash he came across was in the form of copper and silver coins, which from time to time, he'd thrown onto the table or kitchen work tops, to lighten his pockets when he'd come home from nights out. Danny scrabbled about gathering up one and two pence pieces, the odd five, ten and twenty pence coins until he had three pounds and some copper. Then he stared at the pittance in front of him and promptly burst into tears.

Danny owned very little, his car was leased and his home including most of its contents were rented. True, he wore designer clothes, diamond cufflinks and the obligatory Rolex watch, but apart from these few items, he had nothing to show for his father's life's work.

As far as he could figure out, he had only two choices, either he had to get Delectra to reinstate their contract and pay in advance for their orders or he had to extricate money from his father. The first option wasn't even a long shot it was out of the field. So what would it take for his father to throw him a lifeline? He'd tried asking him for help only to be unceremoniously ejected from his home by a Neanderthal, but, he wondered, would his father stand aside and actually let him die?

Danny made his way through to the bathroom and opened the medicine chest. He stared into the jumble within then gathered together all the packets of tablets he could find. There were several opened containers of aspirin, paracetamol, ibruprofen and many loose tablets of indeterminate origin. He carried the whole lot into the lounge and dropped them onto the coffee table then he lifted a pen. On the back of one of the many 'final demand' letters he'd received, he began to write his suicide note. Not that Danny planned to kill himself, quite the reverse in fact. His plan was to save his life.

The note was carefully worded, aimed at his father and designed to tear at the heart strings. It was contrite, apologetic and above everything else, loving. He planned every detail of his 'suicide' in such a way as to cause himself the least harm and inconvenience, yet have the most impact and hopefully the desired outcome. He staged it well, placing empty alcohol bottles all around where he lay on the sofa and emptying the various packets of pills, spilling them onto the coffee table and floor beside him with a generous helping scattered over his torso. Then, clutching the suicide note, Danny swallowed only two paracetamol and two aspirin before dialling 999.

"Help me, please help me," he begged the emergency operator who answered his call. "I don't want to die."

CHAPTER 24

The Rigby children were annoyingly exuberant first thing that morning.

"Quiet guys, please," Johnny pleaded. "I can't hear myself think."

"How can you hear yourself think, Daddy? You think in your head not out loud," Emma replied.

"Not out loud," Alex echoed.

"Children, that's enough now," Bee cut in. "Daddy's tired and he's got to get ready for work. Have you got your gym kit, Emma? Is your bag packed, Alex? Where's Marie?"

"She's trying to find Alex's reading book. He hid it," Emma giggled.

Marie came into the kitchen triumphantly clutching the book. She wagged her finger at Alex. "You are a cheeky menkie," she said, not getting the pronunciation quite right.

"Menkie, menkie, cheeky little menkie," Emma chanted clapping her hands and dancing in time to her singing.

"Enough," Johnny cried holding his hands in front of him defensively. "If you don't be quiet they'll be no pocket money for the picnic."

For a split-second both children stopped bouncing around and Emma made a gesture of zipping her mouth closed. Then they both looked at each other and burst out laughing.

"We'll leave early for school and walk slowly," Marie offered. "Then you'll get some peace and quiet."

Johnny smiled at the au pair, "Do you know you're a treasure?" he asked.

"A treasure like pieces of eight, like pirate's treasure," Alex quipped.

"Go," Bee replied laughing. "You're much too smart for your own good, young man."

With a bustle of bags, blazers and kisses the children were ushered out of the house by Marie and the door closed behind them. The silence that ensued was palpable.

"Phew," Bee said, "That was exhausting. It's always the same when a school holiday is imminent and of course the picnic is just adding to their excitement."

"This picnic seems to have grown legs. It was never meant to be such a big event. It started off being a company event and now the whole district is involved."

"Yes, Darling, but think of all the free advertising Rigby's is getting. That kind of publicity would cost a fortune. I wouldn't be surprised if the TV companies covered it too. Everybody's talking about it."

"I hear what you're saying and you're absolutely right, but still, I'll be glad when it's over."

Johnny glanced at the kitchen wall clock. "I'd better get moving. I'm not looking forward to this morning. The accountants are bringing me their findings on Eddie Maxwell and I'm pretty sure they'll have discovered he's been ripping me off."

"Oh no, how awful," Bee replied her face full of concern. "What will you do? He's a family friend."

"He was a family friend when my dad was alive. He's no friend if he's been stealing from me. Anyway, Pet, I'd better get going and face the music. I hope our little menkies will have calmed down by the time they get back from school," he added laughing.

The drive to work was tortuously slow because a lorry had shed its load in the town centre and not just any load, but empty gas cylinders. They had rolled off the back because the gate holding them in place wasn't properly secured. Once in motion, the heavy cylinders caused all sorts of chaos as they tumbled and bounced into cars and buses and littered the road and pavement.

Johnny called the office using his voice-activated hands free. Elizabeth answered, "Hello, Rigby's. How may I help you?" she asked.

"Hi, Elizabeth, it's me, I'm stuck in traffic and I'm going to be late. Possibly up to an hour. Let Theo know when he gets in, please."

"Of course, Mr Rigby, I'll inform Mr. Walker. Oh, and Eddie Maxwell has phoned for you twice. He says it's urgent. He won't tell me what he wants and he won't speak to anyone else."

Johnny felt an icy lump form in his chest, a heavy sadness. "Just keep saying that I'm not in the office if he calls again. In fact tell him I'm not expected in today."

"Yes, Boss, okay," she replied. Johnny could hear the doubt in her voice, but he wasn't in the mood for explanations.

When he ended the call, Johnny phoned the Walker residence. Mandy answered on the third ring.

"Hi, Mandy," he said. "Is Theo there or has he left for work?"

"He left ages ago. He should arrive any minute." Her voice was flat and unemotional.

"Good, it's you I want to talk to," he replied. "We haven't spoken for a few days and I think we should discuss our situation. I don't want our friendship to be damaged. We had a fling and it was great. I think you'll agree we were good together, but it's over now. I love my wife and you love your husband and then there are our children to consider. All good things come to an end, don't they?"

Johnny was rambling, he knew he was, but he was nervous.

"So can we go back to how we were before? When we're at the picnic can we act as normal and forget it ever happened? For the sake of our families," he added.

Mandy listened in silence. She felt cold and detached. What a prick, she thought. How could I ever have wanted him? Without saying a word, she replaced the receiver and ended the call.

Johnny sighed with relief. "I guess that's a 'yes' then," he said aloud.

When he eventually made it in to work the office was in chaos. One typist had phoned in sick, another had been stuck in the same traffic jam as Johnny and was yet to appear and Colin had telephoned to say that the VIP he'd been sent to the airport to collect, a senior manager from a Chinese supplier, was going to be delayed by at least three hours because of a technical problem. Poor sod's company probably made the faulty part that's causing the delay, Johnny thought caustically.

"Eddie Maxwell has phoned again, the canapés haven't arrived for your meeting with suppliers, Tom and Mr Walker both want to see you and I either need some assistance or tomorrow off if I'm to get everything sorted out for the charity event," Elizabeth said as soon as she saw him approach.

Elizabeth's desk was cocooned in paperwork. There were files in heaps on the floor and post it notes adorned every surface. She looked frantic.

"Tomorrow's the last working day before the month end. Is all your work up to date?" he asked.

"Yes, Boss, it's just the picnic that's causing me grief. The logistics are impossible for one person to deal with. My friend Eva has been helping me but it's not really her responsibility. I know it's my chosen charity, but it's actually Rigby's event."

Johnny considered what she'd said, "You're right Elizabeth, you're absolutely right, I'm sorry. You're just so good at organising everything I hadn't considered the enormity of the task. I can't really spare anyone at the moment because we're not only short staffed in the office, but in the warehouse too. I'll be able to let you away early tomorrow. I'll just need you here for a couple of hours in the morning and I'll telephone my wife to see if she can give you some support. You know Bee, you've met her several times, she's very efficient when it comes to putting things in order."

Elizabeth exhaled her bated breath with a sigh and visibly relaxed, "Thanks, Boss," she said. "My friend Eva knows your wife too. She told me they attend the same yoga class. I'd be very grateful if you'd ask her."

"I'm on it right now. Dial her mobile number while I get myself a coffee then put the call through to my office. Tell Theo that I'll see him and Tom in fifteen minutes then call Colin for me and ask him to come back here. There's no point in him hanging about at the airport when Mr. Lui is going to be delayed for such a long time. Ask him to stop at Marks and Spencer's on his way back and pick up canapés, enough for eight people, please."

Johnny poured himself a coffee and sat down at his desk to await the call to Bee being switched through. He rubbed his face with his open hands, his head was buzzing, full of too much information and it was still only ten in the morning. The day loomed long. He was already tired and feeling as if he'd done a week's work.

CHAPTER 25

When Jenny brought Joe home from school Neil was already in the house.

"You're early, is everything okay?" she asked.

"Fine," he replied flatly. "I just needed peace to think."

Recently, Neil had been working from home more frequently. Jenny was concerned, he was normally so sociable and although his work was mostly done by computer and phone, more often than not, he chose the environment of the company's office so he could interact on a personal basis with his colleagues.

"Mummy and I walked home from school with Ben and his Mummy," Joe said excitedly. "Ben is my best friend and guess what, his daddy is called Wolfie, isn't that a cool name? Maybe he's a superhero. He probably changes into the Wolf Man. Ben said he's an optican and he fixes people's eyes. Maybe he's got x-ray vision when he wears his superhero clothes. Maybe he doesn't wear any clothes except for underpants because wolves have fur. He'd have to wear underpants or it would be rude."

"Optician not optican," Jenny corrected. "Wolfie is German," she explained to Neil, "And from the look of him about as far from being a superhero as possible," she laughed. "He's short, slim, shy and bespectacled. His wife Esther is tall, plump and loud, nice girl, but the poor man doesn't stand a chance. She definitely wears the trousers in that household."

"No Mummy, you're wrong. Ben's mummy was wearing a blue dress today and a baseball cap and big, army boots. I think maybe she's a superhero too. Maybe Ben will grow up to be a superhero and I'll be his helper and help him save people in danger and we'll save the world from space invaders."

Neil's face broke into a grin, "We can't have too many superheroes, my man. You stick in there."

Jenny made coffee for her and Neil and poured juice for Joe then they sat together at the kitchen table chatting and snacking on digestive biscuits.

"Ben gets chocolate biscuits for his snack," Joe said.

"Good for Ben," Jenny replied. "Well, when he comes here to play after school I'm afraid it will be digestives or nothing."

Without further protest Joe quietly reached for a second biscuit and gently lifted it off the plate.

"Ben lives beside Albany House at the end of the road, Daddy," he said changing the subject. "He said it's been sold to two old men and they've got a swimming pool and they told Wolfie we could swim in their swimming pool and play in their big garden any time we wanted."

"You've not to call Ben's daddy Wolfie. It's Mr. Merkel to you," Jenny chided.

"Do you know the name of the people who are buying Albany House?" Neil asked Jenny.

"Esther said one is called Goodheart, funny name, same as the Home, easy to remember, don't you think? I can't remember the other one though, something simple like Smith."

More likely Jones, Neil thought. He felt his blood run cold. He stood up abruptly and knocked against the table, rattling crockery.

"I'm going up to the study to work," he muttered. "I don't want to be disturbed."

Shaking and sweating, he practically crawled up the stairs. His limbs felt leaden and he had a banging headache. Anger burned and seethed inside him at the thought of that monster moving into his street.

Since talk of the picnic had begun Neil couldn't sleep at night, he felt as if insects were crawling inside his skin, he couldn't eat properly, when he tried to swallow bile rose acidly in his throat, everything tasted strange to him. Even the air he breathed smelled foul. All his thoughts were tainted, poisoned by Stanley Jones. He couldn't bear the thought of that vile monster and his cohort Goodheart receiving accolades at the picnic. Nobody knew what they were really like because every child they'd harmed was still terrified of them. Worse still, he had to listen to his beloved sister going on and on about the Goodheart Home. He'd been so terrified and tortured in that place. God knows how many other little boys had been damaged there. All his life he'd been afraid, but he'd managed to avoid any contact with Jones. Now he was incensed. Jones had been in his street, he'd had the audacity to look at his son. Now he was going to move in. Would he come here, knock on the door, perhaps when Neil was at work? What if Joe was on his own playing in the garden? What if he took Joe away in his car? Since seeing Jones drive past, horrifying visions plagued his waking hours and paralysing nightmares had him screaming out in his sleep. He couldn't go on this way. Neil had to confront his demons. He had to kill the beast.

For hours he did nothing except sit at his desk with his head in his hands and think. Eventually, he had a plan. With shaking hands, he reached for the phone and punched in Elizabeth's number.

When Elizabeth arrived home from work and received the call it took her by surprise, a very pleasant surprise.

"Hi, Sis, it's me. Sorry I've not been in touch, but I've had a few things to deal with."

"Neil, I'm so pleased to hear from you. Is everything okay?"

Neil hesitated.

"Neil, Neil, are you all right?"

"Yes, I'm fine. At least I will be after the weekend. There's been a change of plan. Jenny, Joe and I will be coming to the picnic after all. Is that okay?"

"Great, yes, fine, I'm so pleased you're able to come and Chrissie will be delighted."

Elizabeth didn't risk asking what had caused the change of plan she was just thankful for small mercies.

CHAPTER 26

When Johnnie phoned Bee to tell her he'd offered her assistance to Elizabeth, she was not at all happy about it.

"The children are off school tomorrow because of the holiday weekend and I had other plans. You should have at least asked me first. You always assume I have nothing else to do with my time," she admonished.

"Babe, I'm sorry, you're right, I should have asked you first, but come on, I need you. I'm drowning under work. Elizabeth's friend Eva Logan, the girl you meet at yoga, will also be there."

She had nothing against Elizabeth in fact she rather liked her. If circumstances had been different, if she hadn't been Johnny's secretary, they might have become friends. Bee admired Eva Logan and that was one friendship she wanted to court. The more time she spent in her company, the more she liked the girl and she was sure Johnny would get on well with her husband, Angus. From what Eva had said about him the two men seemed to have a lot in common.

Bee was becoming more and more irritated by Mandy Walker. Over the years she had moved forward whereas Mandy was simply marking time and Bee now realised just how shallow and vapid Mandy was.

Perhaps this opportunity to volunteer alongside Eva wasn't such a bad thing after all. It might help her to build a new friendship.

"You know this is going to cost you big time, Johnny, don't you?"

"I don't doubt it for a single moment and I've got a peace offering," he replied. "Do you remember I said that the weekend after this I was going to be away at a trade event?" Bee didn't respond. She'd experienced these 'trade events' before. When Johnny returned from them he was always hyper and she was sure they were cover-up stories for his occasional affairs. "Well," he continued, "As it turns out, I don't have to go after all. With the Delectra order we'll be working at full stretch for the next few months, at least until we figure out how to expand the working day, so there's no need to tout for more business. We'll be able to go out with Theo and Mandy and have some fun instead."

Great, Bee thought, more time chatting about inane rubbish with Mandy while the boys talked shop.

"I'm pleased you have the time off, but don't make any arrangements with Theo. I see you've forgotten I'm going to Prague with my sister. I do have a life you know."

Great, Johnny thought. No awkward chit-chat with Mandy and less chance of her to putting her foot in it. A bit of distance between us will be no bad thing until everything settles down.

"Sorry, Darling, my head's all over the place. I completely forgot about it."

Before Johnny ended the call he'd told Bee that he'd be late home as there were some things he had to discuss with Theo about Eddie Maxwell, so once again she'd be spending dinner alone with Marie and the children. On this occasion, however, she didn't make a fuss because Johnny had sounded so sad. He'd known Eddie for a large part of his life and, from what Johnny had told her, he had a very difficult task ahead.

Rather than sit in the house, once school was over, Bee and Marie took the children to McDonalds for a fast food meal. It was a rare treat for them because even with the company's assurances about having a low salt content, and the inclusion of salad and fruit on the menu, Bee didn't entirely trust the food to be a healthy option. Nevertheless, the children were delighted.

"Chicken nugget happy meal with fries and a cola," Emma said.

"Burger happy meal with fries and a cola for me," Alex said and he galloped round the queue unable to contain his excitement. "Don't forget my toy," he added.

"Stand still, Alex. You're bumping into people," Bee pleaded.

"I thought it was you," a voice from behind her said. Bee turned to see Mandy. "Charlie and I are sitting over there, beside the window. I'll hold the seats in front of us for you," she offered. "Theo's working late so I thought we'd come here for a treat. I guess great minds think alike."

Mandy was the last person Bee wanted to see at

the moment. She didn't want to spend the next hour gossiping or talking about minor celebrities. She wanted time out from the house and any conversation about Johnny's work.

"Thanks," she replied flatly. "We'll just get our food then we'll come over."

"I'll take the kids and get them seated, shall I?" Mandy offered. "Emma, Alex, come with me. Come and talk to Charlie while Mum and Marie get your food."

Obediently the children followed her. It was a relief to have Alex calm down and stop bouncing into people, but Bee still would have preferred her family to be on their own.

By the time Bee and Marie arrived with the food, Mandy had relocated the children to a table that could seat their whole party together. Emma and Alex began to devour their meals, but first they searched the boxes and located their toys. Most of the conversation revolved around the picnic, but when that subject was exhausted Charlie piped up, "I'm going to scout camp the weekend after this. I'll gain two badges and I'm going to learn to cook on a camp fire. We're not actually going to cook anything because of health and safety. We're just going to learn how to do it."

"What are your plans now you're going to be child free," Bee asked Mandy.

"I did think I was going to have the house to myself, but Theo's business trip's been cancelled so we'll probably spend the weekend chilling out."

"Mum said she was going to go out dancing

with her friend while we men were away, but my Dad doesn't like dancing," Charlie said. "So her friend will just have to dance alone now," he added.

Colour rose to Mandy's cheeks and she turned her face away, but not before Bee noticed. In that moment, in that split-second, Bee knew. She put two and two together and made exactly four. With Theo away, Charlie at scout camp, Johnny supposedly away, Mandy meeting a friend and all this going on while she was due to be in Prague and Marie looked after her children. It was crystal clear, it made perfect sense, Johnny's latest fling, his latest bimbo, was Mandy. Everything had been manipulated so the two of them could spend the weekend together.

Bee stared and stared at Mandy. Tears filled her eyes and she fought to contain her grief. Nothing could ever be the same again. How could Johnny shit on his own doorstep? How could he betray her with his best friend's wife? Mandy looked as if she was going to speak.

"Not a word," Bee hissed. "I don't want to hear it," she warned. "Now is not the time."

With as much composure as she could muster, Bee stood, "My, look at the time," she said making a show of looking at her watch. "Everyone finished? Good, we'd better be going now. Say bye to Charlie, children. You'll see him on Saturday."

Marie didn't miss the looks that passed between the two women. She quickly and efficiently collected their belonging, gathered up the children and ushered them towards the door. She knew something was amiss and was sure that before the night was out she'd know what it was.

The air was hot and heavy as they made their way to the car. Bee was grimly silent. As they headed for home, the atmosphere inside the car was just as oppressive. Bee drove distractedly and aggressively, almost sideswiping a cyclist, seeing him only at the last minute, she screeched to a halt. The shocked young man's jaw dropped and he wobbled alarmingly before racing away from her.

"Bloody cyclists, they shouldn't be allowed on the road," she said, then gripping the wheel, white knuckled, she continued.

Emma chewed at her lips nervously, Alex clutched his 'happy meal' toy in his sweaty little hand and Marie tried to ease off her seat belt which had locked as they'd braked, claustrophobically pinning her to her seat.

"I'll have us home in a jiffy," Bee said with mock cheerfulness. The children couldn't wait to get out of the car and Marie recited a prayer under her breath. After what seemed like a lifetime, but was in fact less than five minutes, Bee turned the car into their driveway. All the occupants let out a sigh of relief.

Once inside the house Bee left Marie to deal with the children and she headed for her bedroom. She checked the time. The office should be closed by now and the switchboard shut down. She took her notebook from her bag and searched for Elizabeth Black's phone number. She had to know if Johnny was really working late or if he had already moved on to another affair.

After making sure the children were downstairs she tightly closed the bedroom door and dialled the number.

"Hello, 5469," a cheerful voice answered. "Who's calling please?"

"Hello, Elizabeth, is that you? Bee Rigby here."

"Mrs. Rigby, hi, Elizabeth speaking. What can I do for you?"

"I thought I'd better touch base with you and let you know I'll be round at about two tomorrow, if that suits you."

"Oh, yes, great, I need all the help I can get," Elizabeth replied, laughing. "It's really very good of you to offer."

It would be if I had been the one volunteering my help, Bee thought wryly.

Instead she said, "Johnny never notices how much work goes on behind the scenes when he's so busy himself. In fact I believe he and Theo are still in the office working late again tonight."

"Yes, they are," Elizabeth confirmed. "I worked until six-thirty then I sent out for pizzas for them. I'd be surprised if they manage to leave before nine o'clock," she added.

Within a couple of minutes of ending her call the phone rang. When Bee looked at the caller display she saw it was Mandy's number and she ran to the top of the stairs.

"Don't answer the phone," she called down. "The call is for me and I don't want to talk at the moment. Just let the machine get it."

Bee listened until the phone rang ten times then she heard the familiar taped voice asking the caller to leave a message after the tone, but she wasn't at all surprised when no message was left.

***

Johnny and Theo worked much later than they'd intended, checking and rechecking the paperwork, documents and figures provided by Tom.

"How the hell did he spirit away so much stuff?" Johnny asked incredulously.

"I'm just as shocked as you are," Theo replied. "The bastard was very clever. He ripped us off in so many ways."

"I trusted him. He was a family friend. How could he do that to me?" Johnny said shaking his head in disbelief.

"It's lucky we checked everything when we did. We can make the Delectra order, just, for this month, but we would have been short for next month's if we hadn't discovered the shortfall. A lot of the cartons we thought were full were actually empty."

"Christ, Theo, what a bloody mess. Eddie could have lost us the entire order. It would have ruined Rigby's reputation."

"What are you going to do, Johnny? How do you want to handle it?"

"Personally, I like to handle Eddie round the throat and squeeze the life out of him, but instead I'll simply fire him. We can't afford any bad press. I just want to get rid of him and hush the whole thing up."

"God, look at the time, it's after ten," Theo said

glancing at his watch. "We'd better lock up and go home. The girls will think we've abandoned them and we need to get some shut-eye so we're ready to handle this situation in the morning. I'll call Eddie first thing and ask him to come in, shall I? I know this is very personal for you. I can deal with him myself if you'd prefer."

"No thanks, Theo. I want to see the bastard squirm. I want to see him try to wriggle out of this. The stealing is bad enough, but I can't forgive the betrayal."

"I couldn't agree with you more. I can't abide thieves and I hate cheats. They're the scum of the earth. I could never do the dirty on a friend."

When Johnny arrived home it was nearly eleven o'clock and the house was in darkness. He was tired so went straight to his dressing room to get changed. As he took off his watch to lay it on the chest of drawers he noticed the envelope with his name on it. He withdrew the handwritten letter it contained and read. 'I know your sordid secret. How could you betray me with Mandy? How could you betray your best friend? You've broken my heart.'

Johnny felt sick to his stomach. Bee knows, he thought, Jesus Christ, she knows. What have I done? Numb with shock, Theo's words came back to haunt him. 'I hate cheats. They're the scum of the earth. I could never do the dirty on a friend.'

CHAPTER 27

THE DAY BEFORE

Johnny spent a fitful night in the guest room then rose, showered and dressed early. He'd tried the door of their bedroom the night before, but discovered that Bee had locked him out. It was understandable given the circumstances. She'd had her suspicions about his dalliances in the past and had always chosen to forgive him and believe the concocted stories he'd offered. Surely this time would be the same. Johnny knew he'd overstepped the mark with Mandy, but Bee loved him, he was sure of that and he expected she'd get over it and forgive him in time. She would never jeopardise the children's home life or their happiness. He left the house quietly, being careful not to wake anyone as he didn't want to have to make conversation. He had other things on his mind which would be just as uncomfortable to deal with.

 Bee heard Johnny try the bedroom door handle the night before and again in the morning. She'd lain awake weeping, only napping for a few minutes occasionally, when exhausted. She was bereft, but she knew they'd have to find a way of moving on. Bee had forgiven Johnny's misdemeanours in the past, but this time was different. This time it was where she lived and she felt humiliated. The two families were due to spend the entire day at the damned picnic the next day. How on earth would she manage to do that she wondered? She didn't know if she could look at Mandy let alone speak to her and what about poor Theo? He didn't deserve any of this. At that precise moment she wanted to punch Johnny's smug face. She wanted to hurt him and make him feel the same pain and humiliation which was tearing her apart.

Johnny drove along the back roads to the office in order to avoid as many built-up areas as possible. He wanted to put his foot down and he was less likely to be caught for speeding going this route. The radio was blaring out a selection of punk and new wave music, the sounds encouraging him to drive even faster. After a ten minute burst he felt calmer, his breathing became steadier and more controlled. He knew he would have to face Theo shortly and he'd have to act as if everything was normal. God, what an ass he'd been. Mandy wasn't even worth the effort. There was a world full of younger, prettier girls who were willing to drop their knickers for the price of a meal and a bottle of cheap cava. But then this was never about the sex. This was about power and control and about proving he was better than the next man. It just so happened, in this case, Theo was the next man.

Johnny pulled into his designated parking space just as Theo was climbing out of his car. He felt a lump form in his throat at the thought of speaking to his friend and he swallowed nervously.

"I see you've come in early too," Theo began.

"I've hardly slept a wink. This is a horrible business to deal with."

The two men fell into an easy pace, matching step for step.

"What time is Eddie due to come in?" Johnny asked pleased to have something other than his own appalling behaviour to think about.

"I've asked him to arrive at nine-thirty. The earlier the better as far as I'm concerned. I just want it to be over. I've been considering who will replace Eddie in the short term and I think one of the floor staff will be able to step up, provided Tom oversees everything."

"Do you have someone in mind?"

"Yes, actually, the lad who's covering at the moment, he's keen and smart and desperate for a chance of promotion. He's got a degree in marketing, so he's no dummy. In fact he'll probably do a better job than Eddie ever did. Eddie is very stuck in his ways. He doesn't like change and with the Delectra order and the planned expansion, everything is going to change."

Twenty minutes after they entered the building Elizabeth arrived for work. She was surprised to see Johnny and Theo were already at their desks.

"I hope we didn't startle you," Johnny said. "I know you're usually the first one in. I'm pouring myself a coffee, would you like one?"

"Thank you, yes. I'm usually first in because I drop Chrissie at her friend's house before eight so they can walk to school together. It's easier to come straight into work than to go home again and it lets me miss the morning rush hour. Even though school's off today for the holiday weekend, my friend Eva is still having Chrissie over."

"I know you're seeing Eva and Bee later, when you finish here. I take it you'll have both girls too. It will be a full household of women so I suppose organising the picnic will be a doddle. Women can multi-task so much better than men," he joked.

"Well, we'll see," she replied. "It depends what time I finish here," she added pointedly.

"I'm expecting Eddie Maxwell at nine-thirty. I don't know when we'll finish our meeting with him, but as soon as he leaves, you can leave too. Just make sure Anita knows she's to answer the phone when you've gone."

"Thanks, Mr Rigby. I can't believe the picnic is tomorrow. It seems to have come around very quickly. At least the weather forecast looks good. Clear skies and sunshine are predicted."

"Good, good," Johnny replied, he hadn't even considered the day being rained off.

The family fun day was scheduled to begin at eleven and finish at four. Johnny was pleased that they'd already arranged to meet the Walkers at ten-forty-five as he couldn't be certain that Bee and Mandy would talk today. He just hoped that tomorrow didn't descend into a cat fight. Bee might, in time, forgive him, but Theo never would so he prayed that he never found out what they'd done.

At nine-twenty-five Eddie arrived at the office.

He was dressed in a black suit, a white shirt which had seen better days and a narrow, black tie. His greasy pony tail was tied up with a thin black ribbon. He wouldn't have looked out of place at a funeral. He approached Elizabeth's desk and grinned, his teeth showing evidence of the toast he'd had for breakfast.

Addressing Elizabeth's breasts he said, "Hiya, Doll, I've an appointment with Johnny at nine-thirty. Will I just go through?"

Elizabeth drew her thin cardigan around her, covering her chest. "Please take a seat over there," she indicated to a row containing four upholstered, wooden chairs. "I'll let him know you're here."

Eddie shrugged, "Okay, Doll, whatever," he replied, and, with his hands in his jacket pockets, he sauntered over to the chairs and sat down.

Elizabeth shuddered involuntarily, no wonder his wife left him, she thought, the man made her skin crawl. She lifted the phone and called through to Johnny's office. Theo was already there.

"Eddie Maxwell's arrived," she stated. "Do you want me to send him in?"

"No, not yet, we're not quite ready for him. Wait fifteen minutes and then show him in." He hung up the phone.

To Theo, Johnny said, "I want to keep him waiting. I want to be the one calling the shots."

Nine-thirty went by, then nine-thirty-five, Eddie approached Elizabeth's desk once again.

"My appointment was for nine-thirty. Does Johnny know I'm here? Have you told him?" He leaned both hands on her desk and hovered over her. Elizabeth felt intimidated by him.

"Please sit down," she said. "I'll let you know when you can go in. He knows you're waiting."

"Oh, does he now?" Eddie replied, pushing back from the desk. He returned to the chairs and sat down heavily.

The minutes ticked by. Finally Elizabeth said, "You can go through now."

"Funny," Eddie said, scowling, "Johnny managed to tell you he was ready without calling your phone. You must be psychic."

Elizabeth couldn't meet his gaze. What a ghastly man, she thought.

Eddie knew something was seriously amiss when he realised both Johnny and Theo were waiting to speak to him. He knew he was in trouble when he took a seat opposite them and saw, laid out on the desk in front of him, were bundles of his fake and doctored order forms. The one from Colin was the latest and it lay on the top of the pile.

Johnny wasted no time. He was raging but managed to keep his voice cold and clinical. Theo interceded stating, "Your letter told you that you had the opportunity of bringing a union official or work colleague with you. Are you waiving that right?"

"Yes, this is between me and Johnny," Eddie replied.

Having anticipated this reaction, Theo pushed a pre-typed sheet of paper towards him and said, "As this is a formal interview, we need you to sign this acknowledging you have waived the right to have your own witness present." Eddie lifted a pen and scrawled across the bottom of the paper. Theo continued, "As you can see we have files showing you have falsified paperwork and misappropriated goods."

Eddie didn't deny it. Instead he smirked, "So what do you think you can do about it?" he replied.

Then Johnny fired him.

"If you want to pursue a case for unfair dismissal, you'll lose," he warned. "I'll make sure you go to jail for fraud and theft. You can walk away now and don't come back. It's entirely up to you. I don't care what you do. I just want you off the premises. I can't stand looking at you for another minute. How could you do this to me?"

Eddie stood pushing the chair away. It crashed to the floor.

"You deserved all you got," he spat, "You always were a spoiled, patronising little shit. I was owed more from you. You would have treated me better if your old man was still alive. Stuff your job. I don't need it and I don't need you. You think you're so fancy, with your big car, big house, posh wife. Well it can go in an instant. You can lose it just like that," he said snapping his fingers. "I'm leaving now, but don't think I'm finished with you. Watch your back. This isn't over."

Eddie strode out of the room and slammed the door behind him. Johnny jumped to his feet but Theo grabbed his arm, "Let him go. He's just letting off steam. He knows you've caught him out."

As Eddie passed Elizabeth's desk she shrank back in her chair.

"You knew, you bitch," he snarled. "You're dead, bitch. I'll get you for this." He slammed his fist on the desk then swept all Elizabeth's neatly arranged possessions onto the floor. "I'll get you," he repeated menacingly.

Eddie stormed out of the building and saw Colin in the car park. He headed towards him.

"The bastards have just fired me," he said.

"Watch out, Sonny Jim, you might be next," he warned. "They showed me your fake order. They know you ripped off the 'blu-rays'."

Colin looked down at his feet unable to meet Eddie's gaze.

"I owned up already," he admitted. "I told the boss I'd made a mistake. I gave him back the machines and he let me off with a warning."

"You fucking, stupid, shit. You've thrown me in it. I covered for you and now I've been fired. You think you're home and dry. Well you're not. I'll get you for this, you fucking, stupid shit."

With that said, Eddie stormed away leaving Colin trembling in his wake.

CHAPTER 28

After Eddie stormed out of the office Johnny and Theo sat in stunned silence for a moment. Then Theo began to gather up the papers from the desk in front of him.

"You were magnificent, Mate," Johnny said, "Calm, cool and collected."

"I was merely following procedure. That is until you fired him, of course."

Johnny closed his eyes and slid his hands down over his face before interlocking his fingers across his belly.

"I'm sorry Theo, but he made me see red. He was so smug, so sure of himself. I couldn't help myself. I thought I was rather restrained. I really wanted to hit him."

Theo's face broke into a smile. "He was smug, wasn't he? And he tried to play that old record again of being your father's best friend. Was he your father's best friend?"

"My father had lots of friends. As far as I know none of the others stole from him or his family, but then you never know," Johnny replied bitterly. "I don't know how you managed to keep your cool, Theo, it's lucky you're not a hothead like me or we'd really be in the proverbial shit."

"Mandy says I'm a cold fish, but sometimes you

have to be when you're working."

At the mention of her name, Johnny felt a stab in the heart. He'd managed to forget what he'd done while they were dealing with Eddie, but now it came rushing back.

"I'd better let Elizabeth go home now," he said changing the subject.

"Yes," Theo agreed, "We can manage now without her and I'd better let her know that all we need is the layout for the picnic and the list of who is doing what, where. I've arranged a team of co-ordinators for the day, a company called Event Planners. They're a new, young company. They really want to be associated with our charity bash so they've kept their costs down."

"Is their price on top of what we're already paying?"

"No, it's included."

"Great, well done, this event is costing a fortune as it is. I'd have been cheaper just giving a lump of money as a donation."

"Maybe, but you couldn't have afforded the publicity we're getting and all the staff and their families think you're putting on a special party just for them. The goodwill is priceless."

"Incidentally, Theo, did you mention to Elizabeth that she doesn't have to work on the day? Does she know you've hired Event Planners? She seemed rather frantic when I spoke to her yesterday. I bet she thinks she's to run the whole thing herself."

"I didn't specifically tell her, but surely she must

realise we wouldn't expect her to take on the sole responsibility. She couldn't possibly manage it. I'd better speak to her right now."

When Johnny and Theo approached Elizabeth's desk they found her weeping. Her belongings were still scattered on the floor where Eddie had swept them.

"Elizabeth, are you all right? What's happened? Did Eddie do this? He didn't hurt you, did he?" Johnny placed his arm around her shoulders to comfort her while Theo gathered up her things.

"He didn't touch me. He just gave me a fright, that's all. He's a horrible, horrible man," she replied, mopping her eyes with a sodden tissue. "I'll be okay in a minute. I'm just a bit stressed. It's my own fault. I've taken on too much. I'll feel better once the picnic is over."

Gently, Theo explained about Event Planners. "Once you email them the information and talk over the details with them, your work is done. Then on the day, all you'll have to do is carry out introductions and they'll do the rest."

Elizabeth began to weep again, "I had no idea. I've put together a team of volunteers, but I still didn't know how we'd cope, they'll be delighted that they don't now have to work. I'll just need to go over my paperwork and plans one more time, and with Eva and Mrs Rigby's help, it will take me only a couple of hours then I'll be able to email everything to the event company. Thank you, Mr Walker. Thank you so much."

"I'd like you to give me the names of your

volunteers," Johnny said. "They're obviously employees who are prepared to go that extra mile. At the very least I want to send them a letter of thanks and praise their commitment to the company. You get off home now, Elizabeth. You've done enough work here today." Johnny took a twenty pound note from his wallet and handed it to her. "Please give this to Chrissie," he said. "Tell her to spend it at the picnic and tell her I'm sorry for stressing out her mum."

Elizabeth tried to protest, but Johnny would have none of it. There were lots of things in his life he had to make amends for and he had to start somewhere.

***

After Johnny had left for work that morning Bee rose from her bed. She then heard further movement in the house a few minutes before nine o'clock. It never ceased to amaze her that during the school holidays the children rose early and were raring to go, yet during term time she had to prise them from their beds. She listened at the door and she could here that Marie was attending to their needs. Bee stayed quietly in the safety of her room. She wasn't yet ready to face the world. She had to think what to do and what to say. She wanted to tackle Mandy before she did anything else. After a few minutes Bee heard muffled sounds from outside the bedroom door and the handle was gently turned.

"Mummy, are you awake? Do you want a cup of tea?" Emma's loud whisper asked.

Bee didn't speak or move, imagining her kind daughter with her ear pressed up against the door, craning to hear if there was a reply. After a few seconds she heard the child descend the stairs calling out as she reached the bottom.

"Mummy's still asleep."

Now feeling free to move around without being overheard, Bee sat at her dressing table and peered at herself in the mirror. Her eyes looked tired both from lack of sleep and from crying. She lifted a bottle of treatment from her table and gently sprayed her face, praying that it did exactly what it promised on the label. Surprisingly, her twenty-five pounds purchase hadn't been a waste of money as her face instantly felt refreshed and brighter. Then she brushed her hair, carefully applied her make-up and dressed in her most expensive, designer blouse and skirt.

"Remember who you are and the position you have," she said aloud to her reflection. "Mandy is an employee's wife, a common little slut with no respect for anybody, not even herself, especially not herself. She's back on the reject pile and you are top dog," brave words from someone who in reality felt bereft and broken.

Now prepared and in the right frame of mind, she was ready to call Mandy and clear the air.

When the phone rang Mandy instinctively knew who'd be calling. She supposed that enough time had elapsed for Bee to get over her shock and be ready to talk. She glanced at the caller ID and saw her suspicions were correct. For a moment she wondered whether she should just let the machine answer, but she knew she'd have to face the music at some time and sooner rather than later could mean damage limitation.

"Hello," she answered hesitantly.

"I have something to say to you. I take it Charlie can't overhear this call," Bee said.

"He's in the garden with his friend, so it's okay to speak."

Bee began, "I am not excusing Johnny's behaviour, not for one minute, women have always been his weakness, the sluttier the better it seems," she added cruelly. "But I considered you to be my friend and not merely the wife of one of our employees. I thought I could trust you and you've betrayed that trust."

She paused but Mandy said nothing, she was trembling and didn't trust herself to speak without crying.

"We're going to be forced into each other's company tomorrow at the picnic," Bee continued. "You may speak to Marie and you may speak to my children. You will not speak to Johnny unless you're asked a direct question. I don't want to hear your inane comments and I don't want you to strike up a conversation that includes me. Do I make myself clear?"

There was no reply. Tears were coursing down Mandy's cheeks.

"Our friendship is over. I don't want to hear you suggesting we share evenings out or weekend breaks or any of the things we did before. What you tell Theo is entirely up to you, but if he ever finds out what you've done, I'll make sure Johnny fires him. Be perfectly clear, Johnny will always choose me and the children over anybody else, besides I'm a director of the company and I have a say in what happens."

Mandy was now audibly crying.

"Do you understand what I've just said?" Bee demanded.

"Yyes," Mandy stammered and before she could say anything else, the line went dead.

Bee was shaking when she ended the call, but she felt strong again. She left her room and made her way down to the kitchen.

"Mummy," Emma said, "You've slept for ages."

"Ages and ages," Alex repeated.

"Well it is the holidays," Bee replied, ruffling Alex's hair. And to Marie she said, "Is there any tea left in that pot? And how about some toast, I'm starving."

After spending the morning with Marie and the children visiting the ice rink, they all came home for lunch and a rest.

"I have to go and help Johnny's secretary to get things ready for the event tomorrow. I'll just be a couple of hours I expect. Both children have been invited to their friend's homes this afternoon and once you've delivered them you're free until they've to be picked up again," Bee said to Marie.

"Thanks Bee, I want to write a couple of emails to my family and send them some photos so they know I'm okay. It always takes me ages because I never know what to say. A bit of peace and quiet will help. Alex is just a little boy but he has so much energy and such a loud voice."

Bee laughed, "I know exactly what you mean," she agreed.

***

When Elizabeth opened the door for Bee she was very pleased to see her. She was almost an hour later than expected and most of the work was finished, but it was her being there rather than her contribution that thrilled Elizabeth. She led her through to the kitchen where the others were already seated and quickly ran through the introductions.

"This is my friend Eva who I believe you've already met."

Eva held up her hand and gave a small wave, "Hi, there," she said.

"Eva's daughter Becky and my girl Chrissie," Elizabeth continued. "We've stopped for some refreshments. Would you like a coffee?"

Chrissie signed, "We've got cake, chocolate cake," and grinned. "You might have to fight my Mum for some though, it's her favourite."

Becky interpreted, "Chrissie offered you some chocolate cake. Would you like a piece? She said you might have to fight her Mum for some. Elizabeth's got a very sweet tooth," she added.

Bee hadn't realised that Chrissie was profoundly deaf. Johnny hadn't said anything. She felt uncomfortable being the only person in the room who didn't understand sign language. It was as if she was the one with the disability.

"Would you tell Chrissie, I'd love some," she

replied.

"You just told her yourself," Elizabeth said. "Chrissie reads lips expertly. So watch out if you think you're having a private conversation. This girl is like 'Hawkeye', she picks up on everything."

After a further hour of working together the task was complete and the women could relax. Bee was enjoying her afternoon. She hadn't realised what a strain socialising with Mandy had been until she'd experienced spending time with these well-educated women. They spoke about current affairs, the history of their town, education in Africa and all manner of other interesting topics. What a difference from being limited to chats about minor celebrities or voyeuristic game shows. Even Chrissie and Becky, young as they were, contributed.

"This has been fun," Bee said. "We'll have to get together again sometime."

"We'll all be at the picnic tomorrow," Eva replied. "I can't wait to see the fancy dress race for the men. I don't know who dreamt that one up, but from what I've heard, it should be hilarious. Some of the girls have been discussing what their partners are wearing, and the costumes range from the ridiculous to the bizarre, everything from a belly dancer with an enormous belly to a 'dalek' wearing a grey, plastic dustbin."

"What's your husband going as," Becky asked Bee.

"I'm not sure," she replied. "We haven't discussed it, but my children will have some ideas."

Bee was pretty sure Johnny hadn't planned to take part. He wouldn't want to spoil his suave image. He wouldn't want to risk looking stupid in front of Mandy she thought bitterly. She'd managed to put her earlier upset out of her mind, but now it all came flooding back, her face became strained and her eyes became watery. She turned away from the group to try and regain her composure.

Noticing her discomfort Eva said, "Now that the work is finished, I'll take the girls round to my house. Becky has to put the finishing touches on her entry for the decorated cake competition. They can have dinner at mine and Angus or I will bring Chrissie home later."

The girls excitedly packed some bits and pieces then they left with Eva in a flurry of goodbyes and kisses on cheeks. The house seemed quiet when they'd gone.

Elizabeth poured two coffees then said, "Do you want to talk about it, or is it a private matter?"

"That noticeable, huh?" Bee replied.

"Look, I saw you were upset, but it's really none of my business. We can change the subject if you want."

"It's nothing major, nothing I can't handle, just a couple of small things that together seem bigger than they really are. A friend upset me then Johnny and I had words, the children were noisy, the car needs a service. You know what it's like. Sometimes things get on top of you. That's all. I'll get over it."

From Bee's list of 'small things' Elizabeth heard 'a friend upset me then Johnny and I had words'. Poor cow, she thought, I bet her husband's let her down. He's got a reputation for having a wandering eye. I wonder who the 'friend' was.

Just then the doorbell rang.

"I wonder who that is, I'm not expecting anyone."

"Probably a sales call," Bee offered.

Bee followed Elizabeth into the hallway and when the door was opened William was standing there. He stepped straight into the house without being invited.

"I've come to see Chrissie," he said aggressively. "Where is she? I want to take her out for dinner."

On noticing Bee his demeanour changed. Sidestepping Elizabeth he said, "Hi, I'm William, Elizabeth's husband."

"Ex-husband," Elizabeth corrected. "Chrissie's not here, she's at her friend's house for tea. You didn't tell me you were coming round. I had no idea or I'd have kept her here to see you."

"You told me she was off school today. I finished work early especially so I could take her out. You keep going on about me not spending enough time with her. I didn't realise I had to make an appointment to see my own daughter," he added bitterly.

"Oh, for goodness sake, William, she's not two years old, she makes her own plans. At the very least she needs to know when you're going to turn up. You can't just arrive out of the blue and expect her to be waiting."

William's expression was dark and angry. His hands were balled into fists. Bee felt uncomfortable but stood her ground not wishing to leave Elizabeth exposed and alone.

William sighed, "Tell Chrissie I'll see her tomorrow at the picnic assuming you haven't spirited her away somewhere else. I have to work in the morning, but I'll find you in the afternoon. I'll call your mobile. Make sure it's switched on. I don't want to be traipsing all over the park looking for you."

Without a word of goodbye, William turned and left.

"I guess we've both had words with our husbands now," Elizabeth said shutting the door and heading back towards the kitchen. "Sometimes I really hate men. They can be so unreasonable."

"Aint that the truth," Bee replied bitterly.

CHAPTER 29

Carlotta reclined in the beautician's chair, stretched out her long legs and admired her newly painted toenails. Then she held her left hand out in front of her, extended her slender fingers and smiled at her matching red fingernails.

"Good job, Nancy," she said to the nail technician. "The colour's perfect. It's an exact match for the dress and sandals I'll be wearing tomorrow at the picnic.

"Can I look at the dress and sandals again Mrs. Donatelli?" the girl asked.

"Sure, help yourself."

The girl lifted the scarlet coloured dress from its bag and laid it across the empty chair which stood beside Carlotta's then she took the matching, strappy sandals from their box and placed them beside it.

"Wow, you're going to knock them dead in that outfit. The colour is sensational against your black skin. What's your husband going to wear?"

Carlotta grinned, "Yellow," she said, "He's going to wear a yellow T-shirt and yellow cut-off shorts."

"Mmm, I see, yellow," Nancy replied. "Well at least he won't clash with you."

The two women exchanged glances then began

to laugh.

"I know, I know," Carlotta giggled. "He's going to look like a plump, ripe banana, but he thinks it'll be the right look for this picnic. Lots of the men will be wearing fancy dress, it seems, but I drew the line at that. It's just not dignified for the head of a large company. What if the press photographed him?"

"Well at least they won't miss him dressed in yellow. You'll both stand out at the picnic, but I'm sorry to say only one of you will be gorgeous."

The women chatted for a few minutes more while ensuring Carlotta's nails were fully dry. Then her shoes and dress were packed back into their bags and she went to the front desk to pay.

"Would you like to purchase any items today, Mrs. Donatelli?" the receptionist asked. "If you like the nail polish you're wearing, we have it on sale at the moment for just twelve pounds instead of fifteen. If you spend twenty pounds you'll also get this hand cream for free," she added, holding up a tube of the product.

"I will take the nail polish, thanks, what other colours are on offer? I'll choose something for my friend Jean. I'm meeting her for lunch."

Opting for a soft pink for Jean, Carlotta paid her bill and made her way to the vegetarian restaurant where they were due to meet, unable to resist popping into an accessory shop on the way to purchase a necklace she saw in the window.

The restaurant was busy, but Jean had managed to secure one of only a few tables which were outside.

There were four chairs round the table and one was laden with her purchases. She stood and waved as Carlotta approached.

"I thought we'd be too hot indoors. It feels rather stuffy today. Is this all right?"

"Perfect," Carlotta replied, leaning forward to kiss her friend on both cheeks before sitting opposite her.

Carlotta placed her bags on the other empty chair.

"For once you seem to have more stuff than me," she observed. "What have you bought?"

"Just things to wear at the picnic. Oh, and some Marks and Spencer's underwear for Phil and a couple of bras for me."

"What have you got for the picnic? I bought this dress and these sandals," Carlotta said reaching into the bags and taking out her red clothes.

Jean grimaced, "My how different we are." She removed her purchases from their bags, revealing pink and grey track-suit trousers, matching T-shirt and a pair of pink trainers. "Not nearly as glam as you, but we're going to a park, for goodness sake. I want to be comfortable."

"Well at least your nails can be glamorous," Carlotta said proffering the pink nail polish she'd bought for Jean. "The colour perfectly matches your trainers."

As they ate their food and chatted Carlotta couldn't help thinking that when Jean became a mother she'd probably spend most of her life wearing track suits and going to the park. It saddened her that shopping trips with her friend and impromptu lunches would become a thing of the past. Carlotta had avoided talking to Jean about becoming an adoptive parent, but when there was a lull in their conversation Jean broached the subject.

"I promised Phil I wouldn't say anything so please don't let on I've told you," she began. "But I'm so excited I have to tell someone. We've been sent a profile of a child, a little boy. He looks just like Phil."

Carlotta was taken aback, for a moment she couldn't respond. She was delighted for her friend, but couldn't help thinking, gosh, that was quick. Her life as she knew it flashed before her eyes.

"How wonderful," she managed to say. "You must be thrilled."

"We're over the moon. Within a few weeks, if all goes well, we could be parents."

Carlotta felt hollow inside. A few weeks are all I have left, she thought. It's like a death sentence.

***

Carlo and Phil had been working flat out trying to clear the decks before shutting down their offices for the holiday weekend. By twelve o'clock Carlo had completed his last phone call, closed the file he'd been working on and went to see how his friend was getting on. Phil was on the phone when he looked round the door. He waved for him to come in then held up his hand and mouthed, two minutes. Carlo poured himself some water from the dispenser then sat down on the plush leather armchair to the front of Phil's desk. After five minutes Phil ended the call.

"I thought I'd never get off the phone. Sorry about that but Mr Donnelly does go on rather."

"How are you getting on? Have you done enough work for the day? Can we escape this place?" Carlo asked.

"Yes, all done and dusted, thank goodness. Do you fancy having a lunch together? I know the girls won't be at home. Jean said they're shopping and eating in town. I could book us a table at my golf club, if you'd like."

"Sounds good to me, but perhaps we should drive our cars home first then get a taxi, then we can have a drink or two with our meal?"

"Great plan, and after the week I've had, I might have more than one or two," Phil replied.

"I know what you mean. I'm still upset about Frankels. We've done business with them for years. I'm not bothered about Danny, the man's an idiot, but I'm fond of Victor. It must be hell for him to see his business being ruined. I can't imagine losing our company because of someone's incompetence."

"And I think there's a realistic chance they will lose the company if Danny carries on the way he's been going," Phil agreed. "He's a whinging moaner who blames everyone else for his misfortune. I'm still not sure we've seen the last of him. He might yet try to worm his way back into our good books."

"We might not have seen the back of him, but he's definitely seen the back of us. I would never consider dealing with him again. Maybe we should be looking at forward planning while we're both fairly fit and well. I know we have key man insurance policies in case one of us takes ill or dies unexpectedly, but what will happen when we want to retire? We don't want to work forever."

"You have sons who could inherit," Phil said. "They might want to take over. And who knows, I might become a father soon as well," he added.

"Is there a child available, have you chosen one?"

Phil laughed, "It's not like picking a dog from the pound. You don't get a list of kids to choose from. They try to match the right child with the right parents based on culture, religion, colour and a whole host of other considerations."

"Sorry, Phil, I didn't mean to offend you. I'm just interested. You know I only want the best for you and Jean."

"I know, my friend, I know. I'm going to tell you something, but you mustn't under any circumstances let Jean find out that I told you. We said we'd keep it to ourselves until we knew for sure. They've found a boy who might be a suitable match for us. His name is Peter and he's six years old."

Phil was smiling. His eyes were bright and filled with tears of emotion. "He even looks like me, Carlo. Isn't that amazing? The boy even looks like me."

Carlo was delighted for his friend, but a picture of Carlotta flashed into his mind's eye. How would she feel about this news, he wondered?

CHAPTER 30

Danny Frankel gradually came to and opened his eyes. He stared around at the spartanly furnished bedroom and tried to gauge where he was. He'd woken up many times after heavy drinking sessions to find himself in strange surroundings. Often he was in the home of one of his drinking buddies or sometimes it was an unfamiliar hotel bedroom. Usually, after a few minutes, he remembered how he'd got there. On this occasion, one of the first things he noticed was the small size of the room then, that there were no windows. Oh, my God, he thought, was he in prison? He had a hazy memory of seeing policemen.

Danny swung his legs over the edge of the bed. He felt rough. His tongue was like sandpaper and his head felt heavy as if it was full of water. With a start he realised he was wearing a hospital robe. It was open down the back exposing his body. Shit, he thought, I'm in hospital. He began to check himself for injuries, but found none. Then it all came flooding back.

Danny remembered being rather drunk. He remembered gathering up all the pills and capsules he could find and staging his mock suicide. He remembered dialling 999 and asking for help and the loud bang as the police smashed open his front door. All the details were coming back to him now. As he emerged from his stupor, the previous day's events became crystal clear.

"Danny, Danny, can you hear me?" the paramedic had said. Shouting at him and patting the back of his hand, trying to rouse him. He remembered opening his eyes and seeing his house full of people in uniform, thinking it looked like some kind of bizarre fancy dress party.

How many pills have you taken, Danny?" the voice had demanded.

"Not many," he'd replied.

"We're just going to put this drip in your arm, Danny, okay?" they'd said, "Just to hydrate you."

Danny knew he'd had a lot to drink and the idea of being given liquid intravenously, for some reason, seemed funny. He'd begun to laugh. Danny remembered he'd had difficulty staying awake.

Then the paramedic had said to one of the policemen, "We'd better take him in for his own safety. I don't think he's swallowed many pills. I've counted the ones on the floor and on the furniture and I've accounted for most of the quantity that should have been in the packets. Nevertheless, we can't rule out his intention was to kill himself, but he simply passed out from alcohol consumption first. We'd better take him to the Southern Infirmary.

"Is there someone we can contact for you, Danny?" one of the policemen had asked.

That's when Danny remembered his original plan, the reason for staging his suicide.

"My dad," Danny replied, "Please phone my dad

and tell him I need him. Be sure to let him know that I've tried to kill myself. Ask him to come and get me." Not considering his father's well-being, or the shock the news might cause him, Danny had reeled off Victor's phone number as the paramedics loaded him onto a chair so they could make their way to the waiting ambulance. As they wheeled him out through the broken front door, Danny said, "What about my house? What about all my stuff?"

"Would you like us to get a joiner to secure the door for you or do you want to appoint someone yourself?" one of the policeman asked.

"You get it fixed, please," Danny replied. Then he laughed to himself, there's no money to pay for it whoever does the work, he'd thought.

***

Just then the door of Danny's room opened and two male nurses appeared. One was young, perhaps in his early twenties. The other appeared to be about fifty. Both men were huge, over six feet tall and broad. Danny felt rather intimidated by them.

"I see you're finally awake, Danny. That must have been quite a session you had. You've been out for several hours," the younger man said.

"Where am I," Danny asked.

"You're at the Southern. You have to see a doctor later today then we can probably get you discharged."

"Has anyone called for me? Has my dad been in touch?"

"You'll have to wait and ask the doctor that.

We're just here to check you're okay. Could you manage some food?"

Danny felt hungry. Usually after a drinking session he fancied a fry up.

"Full English, please, Jeeves," he joked.

"Very funny, Son," the older nurse said. "Full English it is then. And would Sir like tea or coffee with that?"

***

When the police came to Victor's door Aggie showed them into the lounge. Both were young and the female officer in particular, looked as if she should still be in school.

"Mr Frankel is not a well man," the housekeeper explained. "If something bad has happened, break it to him gently, please." Then she hurried off to fetch Victor from his study.

When he was first given the news about Danny, Victor sank into a chair. Even though he disliked his behaviour and his incompetence, Danny was still his son and the thought of him attempting to end his life, distressed him greatly.

"Just so you know, Sir," the policewoman said, "The doctor who saw your son was pretty sure there wasn't much wrong with him. His main problem was caused by the amount of alcohol he'd consumed. The doctor thinks he'd only swallowed a couple of pills."

"So he staged this drama to get my attention."

"I'd give him the benefit of the doubt and say he probably didn't know what he was doing in his drunken state."

"You're very kind, Officer," Victor said, "But I'm afraid I find it difficult to be so forgiving. You see my son has pulled stunts like this before. He's a spoilt, selfish, lazy, good-for-nothing and I've washed my hands of him. When will he be released from hospital?"

"He's been left to sleep it off so it'll be a several hours before he sees the doctor again. I'm sorry to bring this news to your door, Sir, but you are his next of kin and he asked us to inform you."

"I'm assuming that now his credit's run out his so-called friends have abandoned him. He wouldn't have wanted anything to do with me otherwise," Victor said bitterly. "Do you have children, Officer?"

"I'm not married, Sir," she replied. "Neither am I," her colleague added.

"Well pay heed to my warning. My son is the product of an overindulgent father. If and when you have children, don't spoil them, teach them the value of money and don't hand them everything on a plate."

"I'm one of nine children, Sir," the policewoman replied. "All of us have had to work for anything we've wanted."

"Perhaps if we'd had more children things would have been different," Victor replied sombrely. "I won't be going to see my son. From what you've said he's not in any danger. He got himself into this mess and he can get himself out of it. I've done too much for him already."

"As you wish, Sir, we just had to inform you. What you do with the information is entirely up to you."

Seeing that Victor looked exhausted Aggie said, "I'll see you out, Officers." As she showed them to the door she was close to tears. "Mr. Frankel senior is such a good and kind man," she said. "That son of his has broken his heart."

***

Now his head was clear and he was dressed Danny carefully planned what he was going to say to the doctor. He realised it was important for him not to be perceived as a potential suicide. If they thought he was a danger to himself, he would not be signed off from the hospital. He didn't want to have to come for counselling sessions and he didn't want mental illness to appear on his permanent medical records. He tidied himself up as best he could, but wasn't able to shave as the staff didn't trust him with a razor at this stage. He wanted to give a good and coherent impression of his condition and of his state of mind.

The door opened and a nurse said, "Would you please come with me, Danny? The doctor is ready to see you now."

Danny followed him down the brightly lit corridor before being shown into an office. The doctor was a short, bald, bespectacled man. Danny smiled when he saw him. He looks nuttier than me, he thought. After a brief interview and to his great relief, Danny was then taken to the reception desk to be handed his discharge paperwork.

"I'm not sure how to get home," he said to the receptionist. "I don't have any money for a taxi. Can you help me?"

"Where do you want to go?" she asked.

"My dad's house," he replied reeling off the address. "He's an old man and he's had a stroke. He doesn't keep any money in the house, but he's the only relative I've got."

The receptionist looked him up and down trying to gauge his sincerity. Danny met her gaze.

"Take a seat over there Mr. Frankel," she said nodding towards a line of plastic chairs. "I'll see if there's a volunteer driver available to take you."

It took an hour and a half but eventually Danny was conveyed to Victor's house. He thanked the man who then drove off. Danny walked up the driveway and rang the bell. He didn't see Aggie peering down at him from an upstairs window. When there was no answer he banged on the door and shouted through the letter box.

"Dad, it's me, Danny. I'm ill. I've been in hospital. Please let me in."

Aggie descended the stairs and walked towards the front door.

"I know you're in there, Dad. Let me in."

Aggie said nothing. Victor had gone away for a few days so he could avoid this type of confrontation. Aggie's son, Billy, had driven him to the coast to stay with his friend.

"Don't think you can shut me out forever, old man," Danny shouted his voice rising to a scream with frustration. "If I go down, I'll take you with me, I'll take a lot of people with me," he threatened.

Still faced by silence, Danny kicked at the door cursing and swearing before stamping off down the path. Aggie was shaken by his outburst, but delighted that this time the useless, waste of space, didn't get his own way. Serves you right, she said to herself. It's about time.

CHAPTER 31

Lionel Goodheart was sitting at the dining table in the bay window of his private drawing room, when there was a knock on the door.

"Enter," he called expecting one of the children from the home to come in. Instead he was greeted by Mavis who wheeled in a tea trolley laden with food.

"I've brought you some lunch, Sir," she said. "Mr. Jones is on his way. He ordered for you both."

She began to place plates of food on the crisply laundered, white, linen tablecloth. There was fresh, crusty bread, smoked mackerel salads and to follow, slices of apricot and almond tart with a jug of clotted cream.

"Lovely, Mavis, everything looks delicious," Goodheart said licking his lips. Mavis smiled and blushed charmingly.

"Are you and Mr. Jones really retiring, Sir?" she asked.

"I'm afraid so, Dear. All good things come to an end and we're not getting any younger you know, but we're not moving very far away. We're buying a house in the area. So you'll be able to visit."

"I'll miss you, Sir," she said. "I've been here nearly twenty years."

Goodheart peered at the little mouse of a woman

and said, "Really, my how time flies when you're enjoying yourself."

Mavis couldn't meet his gaze, she shyly stared at her feet and her face reddened once again.

Just then Stanley entered.

"I'll leave you two to eat," Mavis said. "Phone down if you require anything else," and with that said she left the room shutting the door quietly behind her.

"Hello Lionel," Stanley said. "I see lunch has arrived, served by the lovely Mavis. A veritable treat."

"Lunch or Mavis?" Goodheart asked and he winked.

"Both, I'm sure," Stanley replied.

"Do you know she's been with us for twenty years? She first came here when she was just sweet sixteen."

"Time for a change, perhaps? Isn't she getting a bit long in the tooth for your taste now?"

"She likes to be restrained during sex, you know," Goodheart said. "She endures all sorts of humiliations. It reminds her of the first time I took her."

"Forced her, you mean," Stanley corrected.

Goodheart smiled, "We each have our preferences, my friend."

"Do you plan to bring her with us to Albany House?" Stanley asked.

"Good God, no, neither her housekeeping nor her skills in the bedroom are that good. Besides, there are plenty of young, Eastern European women willing to bend over backwards for a job that includes a roof over their heads."

"Whatever turns you on," Stanley replied smiling.

The men began their lunch and while eating, they each read their newspapers. When they were finished Goodheart said, "You went out quite early this morning. Did you go somewhere interesting?"

"I took a walk in Albany Road. I wanted to see how busy the street is during school holiday time. There were lots of children playing out on the pavements, riding those little scooters and bikes, or kicking a ball about. They were all very friendly and they chatted away to me."

"I'm glad you like the place because my offer has been verbally accepted." The estate agent telephoned an hour ago. The house is ours."

There was a knock on the door once again and, when invited, Mavis re-entered the room.

"Your post has arrived," she stated handing it to Goodheart. "Shall I clear the table, Sir?"

"Yes, please," he replied.

Mavis began lifting plates back onto the tea trolley. As she reached across the table with her back facing Goodheart he slid his hands under her skirt and fondled her buttocks while Stanley looked on. Mavis froze. Goodheart slipped his fingers inside her panties. She began to tremble. Stanley licked his lips and stared lasciviously. After a moment, Goodheart withdrew his hands and patted her bottom.

"Thank you, Mavis," he said. "Lunch was delicious. You can bring us coffees now."

Mavis adjusted her skirt then, wheeling the trolley now loaded with dirty plates, she left the room.

"You really are a dirty devil," Stanley said.

"Nonsense, she loves it. That was just a little taster of what's to come. She'll be begging me for more once you've gone."

When the two men began opening their mail Goodheart was surprised to see a letter from the Board advising him that he was to receive an award.

"According to this," he began, "Councillor Brown is to present me with a certificate at the charity picnic, commemorating my years of good service to the community."

"A certificate, is that the best they can do?" Stanley replied. "No large cheque or gold watch, just a certificate?"

"It's the honour not the material gain," his friend replied.

Stanley gently tapped his lips with his fingertips and smiled. "I suppose over the years we've already enjoyed our physical rewards," he observed.

CHAPTER 32

SATURDAY – THE DAY OF THE PICNIC

Elizabeth Black woke with a start and stared at the luminous dial of her alarm clock. It was barely six am. She sighed and laid her head back down on the pillow. She'd woken practically on the hour every hour since two, subconsciously worried about over sleeping. She was due to meet up with representatives from Event Planners at nine, so she could walk them round the designated picnic area and introduce them to the various stallholders, contributors, and indeed all the relevant people involved. She reckoned it would take her less than an hour then she'd be free until Mr. and Mrs. Rigby arrived, at ten-thirty.

Unable to get back to sleep, she went over and over in her mind, the timing of everything she had to do until her head was buzzing. At seven-fifteen she rose, switched off her alarm, showered and dressed then she woke Chrissie.

"I have to be at the park very early this morning so I've arranged to drop you at Becky's house on the way. Eva and Angus will make sure you're there in time for the opening."

"What about Dad? When will I see him?" Chrissie signed.

"He's working in the morning, but he said he'd phone my mobile early in the afternoon so I can tell him where to meet up with you."

"Will it be noisy in the park? You said there's to be a DJ, are you sure you'll hear the phone?"

Elizabeth stared at her daughter's anxious expression and her heart felt heavy. She prayed that on this occasion, William wouldn't let her down, but his past record wasn't good and they both knew he couldn't be relied upon.

"Don't worry, Pet, your dad will find you. I promise you I won't miss his call," Elizabeth tried to reassure her.

While Chrissie got herself ready Elizabeth packed a cool bag with food for the picnic.

"When you go upstairs to get your sunglasses fetch the blanket with the plastic backing please, just in case the grass is damp," Elizabeth said. "We don't want to get wet grass stains on our bums, it's not a good look," she added.

When Chrissie returned she was clutching a gift wrapped box which she handed to Elizabeth.

"What's this?" Elizabeth asked.

"For you, Mum," Chrissie signed.

Elizabeth looked quizzical. Chrissie grinned delightedly.

"Will I open it now?"

The child nodded enthusiastically.

Elizabeth carefully peeled off the wrapping paper to reveal a small box of handmade ginger chocolates, her favourites. There was a gift card decorated with flowers which read, 'Well done, Mum. You're a star. I'm proud of you. Love Chrissie, x x.'

Elizabeth felt a lump form in her throat, "Thank you, Darling. How kind of you. This is so unexpected. You've really made my day." She leaned over and kissed her daughter on the cheek.

"I know they're your favourites. You deserve a treat. You've worked so hard on the fun day." Chrissie's eyes shone brightly and she smiled broadly.

"Well, by the time you arrive with the Logans my work will be done and we'll be able to spend the whole day having fun together. On that note, we'd better get going," she added looking at her watch.

After depositing Chrissie at her friend's house, Elizabeth made her way to the park. As she approached she was relieved to see a banner proclaiming 'family fun day, here today' attached to the park railings. Event Planners must have collected it from the office after I left yesterday, she thought, and they must have arrived here today. She drove between the large wrought iron gates of the main entrance and pulled her car into the car park immediately to her left. There were already a couple of cars there and some vans and when Elizabeth read the signage emblazoned on the vehicles, she was delighted to see that all the people who should have been there to set up, had arrived. At last she could relax. She felt as if a heavy weight had been lifted off her shoulders.

***

The man had been studying the internet all night, popping pills in order to stay awake. He was full of rage. He'd been reading about killers. They were ordinary people, just like him. People who'd been treated badly and had nothing left to live for. So many wronged individuals who'd chosen to end their lives in a blaze of glory shooting up the world, while at the same time taking out several of the bastards who'd hurt them and driven them to such despair.

The man liked guns. He collected them. His pride and joy was a Kalashnikov assault rifle known to the west as the AK-47. He was a member of his local gun club and two of his guns were licenced, but not his AK-47 or the Glock he'd modified to be fully automatic. Nobody knew about those guns or the three thousand rounds of ammunition he'd imported.

CHAPTER 33

Johnny rose early having spent a sleepless night alone. He and Bee kept overly cheerful in front of the children, but any interaction between them was cold and detached. From time to time Bee sniped at him unable to hide her annoyance. The children were excitedly chatting about the day ahead. But the frosty atmosphere between their parents wasn't missed by Marie and she tried to break the tension by striking up a conversation with Bee.

"My friend Isobel is going to the fun day with her family. She said we could meet up if that's all right with you," Marie said.

Bee had met Isobel once before and didn't trust the girl to behave herself. Margaret Wilson, the woman who employed her as an au pair, was forever moaning about her antics.

"She's basically a good girl," she would say. "Intelligent, funny, a bit flighty, but also wilful and she has a too healthy appetite for men, not boys, I might add, but men. Lucky my husband Eric is a stuffy old academic. He wouldn't notice Isobel if she stood in front of him butt naked and the way she dresses, sometimes I think naked would be an improvement."

Bee was acutely aware of the responsibility she'd taken on by employing an au pair. They are not quite fully grown up, are a guest in your home, treated like an older child of the household and given pocket money rather than wages. They have their own ideas about what is acceptable and what is not, coupled with this they are at an age when their hormones are raging.

"Isobel is welcome to join us, but your job is to look after Alex and Emma. This is our event. Johnny and I are the hosts and we might be called upon to meet people and take part in things. I have to be able to rely on you today, Marie."

"Of course, I understand what's required. Isobel will come to meet me and not the other way around. You can rely on me. I won't let you down."

After two false starts because Emma and Alex each forgot something, they finally made it to the park. They walked along the short footpath which opened up to a wide expanse of grass, beyond which stood a boating lake.

"Look," Alex shouted excitedly, pointing straight ahead. "They've got a food van. I told you Marie I'd be able to have a dog for my lunch. I might have a burger but I think I'll want a dog. Then for afters, I'm going to get candy floss or maybe ice cream." For a small boy, Alex had a voracious appetite.

"You've just had breakfast, surely you're not hungry now," Bee said.

"Alex," Marie said with exasperation. "We don't eat dogs in Europe maybe in China but not here. Tell him Bee. Tell him we don't eat dogs. Why would you want to eat a little puppy? I told you yesterday you can't eat a dog."

The family stared at Marie for a moment before exploding with laughter.

"What? What have I said that is funny?"

"Hot-dogs, Marie," Johnny explained. "A sausage in a roll is called a hot dog. Alex doesn't want to eat a real dog."

"But he said 'dog' not hot-dog. I'll never understand. Why don't you just say what you mean? It's like trying to untangle a secret code. I thought the cheeky menkie really wanted to eat a dog."

"Monkey, Marie," Bee corrected, "Remember I told you before? Alex is a monkey."

"I'm not a monkey I'm a boy," Alex protested.

"That's a matter of opinion," Johnny replied and they all roared with laughter once again.

As Marie took the children to look at the exhibitors' stalls Johnny and Bee made their way to the marquee which was to house the entries for the various competitions. They'd arranged to meet Elizabeth there, and when they approached, they saw her sitting on a plastic chair outside the entrance sunning herself. She jumped up as soon as they drew near.

"Hello, you're right on time, everything looks great doesn't it? Event Planners have been here since first light. They're a fairly new company but they're spot on. I'm really impressed."

Bee greeted Elizabeth with a friendly kiss on both cheeks while Johnny stood awkwardly behind her.

"If you'd just introduce us to whoever we have to liaise with for the opening speech and prize giving, you can go back to sunbathing until your family and friends arrive," Bee said. "God knows you deserve it after the shed load of work you've put in."

"Thanks Bee, it's really nice to be appreciated."

With that said, both women looked pointedly at Johnny who stared at the ground unable to meet their critical gaze. Once the introductions were made, Elizabeth moved away from the marquee as quickly as she could go. She wanted to distance herself from Johnny and Bee in case she was drawn into helping with further tasks. I'm free, at last I'm free, she thought and she practically skipped her way across the grass.

***

The man swallowed some more pills. He was sweating profusely and his skin stank of body odour, every pore oozed the stench. Rising from his desk, he felt ravenously hungry so he raided the kitchen cupboards gathering up packets of biscuits, an almost empty box of cereal and an out-of-date carton of crackers. Then he emptied the fridge of anything he could eat which didn't require cooking, before carrying it all back to his desk and returning to the computer.

Studying the screen he turned his attention back to massacres which involved firearms. Columbine and Dunblane were prominent, but the man was more interested in cases where work related shootings had taken place, where the injured parties directed their revenge at the right people and their supporters. He discovered so many incidents which he perceived to be justifiable homicides, ranging from 'going postal',

Patrick Henry Sherrill who shot twenty co-workers killing fourteen of them in 1986 to Omar Sheriff Thornton who shot and killed eight people in his former workplace in 2010. In his eyes, in every case, a clever man had been robbed of his livelihood and had nowhere to turn. Justifiable homicides indeed, the man thought.

CHAPTER 34

An employee of Event Planners had placed a tape barrier across the main entrance to the park and a lone person manned the gate. At eleven o'clock the tape would be unclipped and pulled open to allow entry to the 'fun day'. There were other ways to get into the park and if someone was determined, they could insist on passing through this particular gate at any time, it was a public park after all, but people queued good-naturedly and waited patiently.

With Charlie zipping along on his scooter, Theo and Mandy arrived fifteen minutes before eleven and made their way to the head of the queue to speak to the official at the gate. Theo flashed his business card.

"I'm the company secretary," he said. "I'm with Johnny Rigby's party."

Without further question, the barrier was opened to let them pass and Charlie sped ahead, propelling himself down the slight incline. Normally, Mandy would have enjoyed the VIP status that allowed her to jump the queue, but this time was different. She would much rather not be in Johnny and Bee's company at all, never mind being forced to spend the entire day with them as part of their inner circle. These first fifteen minutes before the masses were allowed in to cause some distraction, would be sheer torture.

She looked at her husband's relaxed smile and matched his easy gait as they made their way across the grass. Poor sap, she thought, he has no idea what I've done, no inkling that his best friend has betrayed him. He reached out to take her hand, squeezed it and winked at her and she felt like crying.

"I can see them. Look they've got their blanket right in the middle of the grass. They're keeping us the best spot," Charlie's excited voice called back as he headed towards the Rigby family. He reached the group a couple of moments before Theo and Mandy, threw his scooter onto the grass and plonked himself down at the edge of the blanket beside Emma.

"Hello Enema," he said laughing.

"Don't call me that, Charlie Farley," she replied. Emma was secretly rather pleased to have the attention of an older boy. At the tender age of ten a boy of eleven was a God.

"Hi Theo, Mandy, Charlie" Bee said, staring up at them from her place on the ground. She made no attempt to stand. Marie, who was sitting beside her, looked as if she was about to move to make room for Mandy, but Bee placed a restraining hand on her arm.

"Spread your picnic blanket on the ground beside ours," she instructed, "Then there will be room for everyone to sit round."

Mandy did as she was told. Theo was already engaged in conversation with Johnny, the children were chatting and joking with each other and Bee resumed talking to Marie. Mandy sat down on the grass and busied herself with her picnic hamper. She was on the outside of the group instead of being the centre of attention or even included. For the first time in her life, Mandy felt isolated and desperately lonely.

"I'm going for a walk to have a look round the stalls," she said unable to stand it any longer. "Does anyone want to join me?"

There were no takers. Bee shook her head, but apart from that no-one even responded. Mandy stood and walked away from the group. She felt like a leper. If this was how the whole day was going to be, she'd find some company elsewhere. Surely there'd be someone she knew to talk to. Why should she be ostracised when Johnny was getting off scot free?

Johnny was pleased to have Theo to chat to. He saw how Bee was treating Mandy and saw her walk away, but he couldn't do a thing about it, he couldn't risk it. He was sorry for Mandy and the situation she found herself in, but he had to ignore it, he had to ignore her in order to save himself.

He checked his watch frequently as the minutes ticked by. The gate was now open and the masses flooded into the park in a wave of confusion and noise. It would soon be time for him to deliver his opening speech. Johnny hated making speeches and he'd be glad when eleven-thirty had come and gone and he could relax.

***

Colin Anderson was so happy that things were back to normal with his job. Although he still felt a slight uneasiness about Eddie Maxwell. The man was annoyed with him and Colin didn't fancy his chances if he was confronted by him in a temper. He'd heard through the grapevine that Eddie definitely wouldn't be back working at Rigby's. No second chances for stealing from your employer it seemed. Colin realised he'd been very lucky.

"Are you ready to leave, Colin? Mum and Dad are already in the car. It's after twelve. We want to get a good spot for our picnic," Caitlin's voice demanded as she called from the open front door.

"I'm here," he replied emerging from the kitchen. "We nearly forgot this," he said holding aloft a plastic container. "Your mum would never forgive us if we forgot her ham and cheese pasties. Not after all the trouble she went to baking them."

"Oh, God, you're right, we'd never hear the end of it. Well done for remembering them."

It took them only ten minutes to reach the park and a further fifteen to decide where to sit. Finally they chose a spot close to the marquee and only a short stroll from the chemical toilets.

"We don't want to be too far from the loos," Caitlin's mum, Rhona said to Colin. "You know how often Alan needs to go when he's drinking beer. Are you sure you're okay about driving back? It means you can't have a drink."

"I'm so happy at the moment, Rhona. I don't need any alcohol. I can get drunk on the atmosphere and the ambiance of the day."

"My, my, Son, have you swallowed a poetry book? No wonder you charmed my girl. I always wondered what she saw in you," Alan cut in laughing.

"Watch out, old man," Colin replied good-naturedly. "You'd better be nice to me or you'll find yourself walking home."

"I saw the Rigby's and the Walkers sitting in the middle of the grass," Caitlin said. "Do you think we should go over and say hello? Mrs Walker looks stunning as usual. I don't know how she does it. Mrs Rigby is quite plain by comparison."

"But Mrs. Rigby has class. Mrs. Walker looks like a bit of a tart and, according to what I've heard, she acts like one too. Give me a wholesome, good woman any day," Colin replied.

"Are you saying I'm homely?" Caitlin joked.

"You're beautiful, Darling, inside and out."

"Crawler," she replied.

"Well handled, Son," Alan said and he tapped the side of his nose with his extended forefinger.

Colin thought about saying hello to the Rigby's then decided he'd better leave well alone. He wanted to keep a low profile until the dust had time to settle and his misdeed was completely forgotten.

"We'd better not go over, Pet, I'm not working today and neither are they. I think it would be wrong to intrude. Now then, Alan," he said turning to his father-in-law. "Why don't you and I have a go at the coconut shy? I bet you were a dab hand at lobbing grenades during the war."

"You cheeky beggar," the older man replied. "I'll have you know I wasn't even born during the war, but I bet, even with my wonky eyesight, I'll win a prize before you."

Caitlin and Rhona chatted happily as they watched their husbands set off towards the games area.

"I guess boys will always be boys," Caitlin said.

"And silly old men will always be silly old men," her mum replied.

CHAPTER 35

Elizabeth's boyfriend Patrick and Eva's husband Angus hit it off right away. They acted as if they'd been friends for years. The afternoon was going swimmingly as both families ate together and took part in the various games on offer. At two o'clock the men, each dressed in their costumes, realised that they were both competing in the same heat of the men's race.

"I hope Patrick and your dad get into the final," Chrissie signed.

"I'm sure they will," Becky replied. "Have you seen the state of the other men in their heat? They're a bunch of old codgers."

The girls laughed.

"I wonder what they're plotting," Eva said.

"I hope they're planning to nobble the rest of our group," Angus replied.

"Billy Bunter won't cause us any trouble," Patrick observed, pointing to a man with a waistline like a roundabout.

"Not unless he falls on one of us," Angus said.

"You two are as bad as the girls. It's meant to be a family fun day not the Olympics," Elizabeth chided.

"For you maybe, but for we men, this is serious stuff, isn't it Patrick?"

"Absolutely," he replied. "How stupid would we look if someone like Billy Bunter beat us?"

"Shh," Eva said, "Don't keep calling him that or he'll hear you."

"Maybe so, but he'll never catch us," Angus added and the two men roared with laughter. "He looks ridiculous dressed as a giant baby with that beer belly."

"This from a pink rabbit and a purple fairy," Eva observed.

Elizabeth kept checking her phone, but there was no call from William. Chrissie hadn't asked, but Elizabeth knew she'd be anxious. Notably, there was no sign of Neil either.

The race eventually began ten minutes late with much jostling and pushing. At one point, a short, stocky Dalmation got into a tussle with Spiderman and they had to be separated by a green crocodile. This caused much hilarity and cheering from the crowd of onlookers. In the end, somehow, both Patrick and Angus made it into the first four with the first six going forward to the final race. The girls were ecstatic.

After the heat both families went to the marquee to see how Becky had got on in the cake decorating competition, and to their delight, she'd won the first prize. Her depiction of the Goodheart Home wowed the judges and their written comments stated, 'Unanimous decision, we all agreed, there could only be one winner, outstanding, well done.'

"I've won a Samsung tablet. I can't believe it. I've actually won."

"When does Becky get her prize?" Chrissie

signed.

"The prize giving will begin at three o'clock," Elizabeth replied. "There will be a formal presentation on the stage. Her category will be awarded first, immediately after the men's race final."

At that moment Elizabeth's phone rang and the caller display showed it was William. At last, Elizabeth thought and she turned away from Chrissie's view to answer it.

"I know I'm late, don't bust a gut," he began. No apology or explanation was offered. "Tell Chrissie I'll meet her at three-twenty, at the side of the boating lake, near the wooden jetty. I plan to take her to see the new Batman movie then afterwards we'll go for dinner. Your fun day should be almost over by then, okay. My car will be parked at the rear entrance."

"Hold on a minute and I'll ask her," Elizabeth replied unable to hide her annoyance. "She's here with her friend you know," she added.

Quickly Elizabeth told Chrissie about William's plan. Her face lit up and she beamed. "I'll have enough time to watch Patrick's race and see Becky get her prize before I have to go," she signed. "Tell Dad, great, I'll be there."

Reluctantly Elizabeth delivered the message and hung up the phone. He always lets her down or changes the plan at the last minute, yet still she adores him, she thought bitterly.

They quickly walked back to the makeshift racetrack for the men's final. Elizabeth was thrilled to see Jenny and Joe watching from the sidelines and she went over to speak to them.

"Hello you two, I'm delighted you're here, where's Neil?" she asked.

"Good question," Jenny replied. "One minute he was standing beside me, the next he muttered something about having to see someone and he took off in the direction of the marquee. He's literally just left. I'm surprised you didn't see him."

"I've just come from there, but it was packed with people. I might have missed him in the crowd. Most of the district is here so he's probably chatting to a neighbour or a friend. Anyway, you two are in time to see my boyfriend Patrick and my friend Angus make complete fools of themselves. They're about to compete in this race. Come over and join us. I'm sure Neil will be back soon."

***

Goodheart and Jones were sitting on their fold-up chairs enjoying the sunshine. Not for them a blanket on the grass, much too undignified. Goodheart was practicing his acceptance speech, making last minute alterations here and there.

"It's so tiresome having to wait around until three-thirty just to receive a poxy paper award. And this is the last of our champagne," he added topping up both of their glasses.

"I'm rather enjoying the view," Jones said, his mind and vision focussing on the many children in the park. "In fact, I think I'll take a walk and stretch my legs. I won't be long."

He stood, ran his fingers through his hair,

adjusted his clothes and drained his glass.

From his vantage point, Neil had watched him rise from his seat. When Jones began to walk towards a group of children kicking a ball about he made an excuse to abandon his family and follow him. He felt frantic. He couldn't risk letting the monster out of his sight, not with all these potential victims around and not before he'd had the opportunity of confronting him once and for all.

CHAPTER 36

The man had showered, meticulously soaping himself then similar to many athletes, he'd shaved all the hair from his head and body. He had to be clean and toned, like a soldier going to war. He had to be prepared for the mission that lay ahead. Carefully selecting his clothes, the man opted for the army surplus, camouflage outfit he wore when he went hunting for rabbits. Then he packed his guns into a holdall, slung the bag over his shoulder and stood admiring his appearance in the full-length mirror.

He was going to take charge now and be the master of his own fate. Nobody could stop him. He had the power to reduce those bastards to blood and pulp. Not many people had the stomach for it. Only a few brave men had gone before him. He saluted them, smiling as the image in the mirror returned his salute.

"Into the valley of death," he muttered.

Leaving his home, without bothering to close the front door, he unlocked his vehicle, threw his bag into the boot then climbed into the driver's seat.

"Here we go, here we go, here we go," he chanted in a loud whisper, over and over again, as he drove, just below the speed limit in the direction of the park.

***

The Rigby and the Walker children had enjoyed their day immensely, but as the day wound down they began to get bored.

"There's nothing left to do. When are we going home?" Charlie whined.

"I'm fed up just sitting around," Alex moaned.

"Do you want to come with me and Isobel to the marquee and look at the exhibits before they're removed?" Marie offered, desperate to get away from the group. Isobel had arranged for them to meet up with two boys at three-thirty and the time was going in.

"I don't want to go and look at all that crap," Charlie retorted.

"Charlie said a bad word," Alex piped up expectantly waiting for him to be told off.

"What have I told you about using bad language, Son?" Theo said.

"It's for people who are too stupid to think of something clever to say," Charlie replied sighing.

"Why don't we take the kids out in a rowing boat," Johnny offered. "We can row over to the island and explore. Then at four o'clock we can all go home."

"Great idea," Theo agreed. "Who wants to come with?"

"I'd prefer to go with Marie," Emma said much to Marie's disappointment. For a moment she thought her time was going to be her own. Still one kid was better than three she supposed.

"I've had enough of the boys and rough games," Emma explained. "I'd like to look at arty things, something intelligent," she added glaring at Charlie and

Alex.

"Arty farty," Alex said and he and Charlie giggled.

Emma gave them a withering look.

"Just the boys then," Johnny said standing and they made their way towards the boating lake.

When Emma, left with the older girls, Mandy and Bee remained sitting on the grass. There was an awkward silence. As the girls walked to the marquee Isobel texted on her phone and almost immediately received a reply.

"They'll meet us behind the tent," she told Marie.

"Will you be okay looking round on your own?" Marie asked Emma. "Isobel and I will be just outside having a cigarette."

Emma knew they'd be meeting boys so she preferred not to be in their company. She was hot and tired and she really just wanted to be going home.

"No problem, Marie. You go right ahead," she replied then disappeared inside the tent without a backward glance.

***

The Donatelli's and the McKay's had really enjoyed the day, but whilst Phil and Jean were getting ready to head for home, Carlo and Carlotta decided to enjoy the afternoon sunshine for a bit longer.

"Would you like to get together for dinner later, I'm cooking," Jean volunteered. "I've got some lovely Scottish salmon in the fridge and I can throw together a salad and baked potatoes. Just a simple meal then we can play Canasta if you'd like."

"Not sure about the cards but the food sounds good. Why don't we bring a DVD then we'll have a choice," Carlo offered.

With the arrangements made, Phil and Jean made their way back to the car park leaving Carlo and Carlotta relaxing on the grass. As Jean eased the car out of its parking space the man drove his car in.

"He was in a hurry to get my space," Jean said mildly annoyed. "He almost clipped my wing mirror."

"I know," Phil replied. "There was plenty of room but for some reason he wanted your space."

"Did you see his face? He had such a look of determination. Perhaps he's just a bit of an oddball."

"To tell you the truth, I didn't notice his face because I was too busy worrying about the car."

"The first thing I'm going to do when we get home is pour myself a large glass of chilled white wine," Jean said. "I've had to watch you guzzling beer with Carlo all afternoon and I'm sick of cola."

"That's because it was your turn to drive, my sweet, but I'll tell you what, when we get home, I'll pour you a glass or maybe I'll make it a bucketful, shall I?" Phil replied laughing.

***

"Oh, for goodness sake, Mum, why are we all standing here? I didn't think I'd be spending half my day hanging about outside a chemical toilet."

"Your father's a bit tipsy, Pet. I need Colin to help him along. Once he comes out I'll just nip in for a quick wee then we can all go home."

"The prize-giving will soon be over then there're only a couple of awards to be given and everyone will be going home. If you don't mind, I'd rather stay to the end and hear how much money has been raised," Colin replied.

"I wish your dad would get a move on, I'm dying to go now. Bang on the door Caitlin and see if he's okay."

"I'm not banging on the door. He's not five years old. You do it if you want."

"But he might be ill inside. He might have collapsed."

"And if he has, what do you propose we do? Load the toilet onto a truck and drive him home? Because if he's locked the door, we won't be able to get in."

"There's no need to be snappy," Rhona replied. "She's always snappy when she's had too much sun and she's tired. It was the just same when she was a little girl."

"Oh, for God's sake," Colin said. "If we don't get a move on I'll miss the announcement." He stepped forward and hammered on the toilet door. "Alan, Alan. Are you okay?"

"Of course I'm all right. Can't a man take a shit in peace? I'll be out soon," came his muffled reply.

Colin looked at his watch. "I'm definitely going to miss the awards," he moaned.

***

The Logan's and the Black's clapped enthusiastically as Becky was awarded her prize. Councillor Brown's wife, who handed her the certificate and the Samsung tablet, had been one of the judges of the competition.

"Your theme was very appropriate, my Dear and your cake absolutely delicious. I had to stop myself from devouring the whole lot. Too many of these competitions and I'll be the size of a house," she joked. "We were very surprised to discover that you are just ten years old. Well done, well done indeed, hearty congratulations."

Becky was beaming as she climbed down from the stage.

"I'm sorry you didn't win a prize Dad, or you Patrick, but I'm so pleased with my tablet," she said clutching it to her chest.

Angus and Patrick didn't disgrace themselves being placed fifth and sixth respectively in the race. However, they felt rather stupid now, still dressed in their costumes and Angus in particular, wished he'd brought a change of clothes with him.

"I hope nobody I know sees me walking home dressed as a fairy or I'll never live it down," he said.

Elizabeth glanced at her watch then said, "If you don't mind I want to walk Chrissie to the lakeside so she can meet up with William. Then if you'd like we can go and have a look at the stables before we head for home. I know you love horses Becky and you can actually go into the yard and see them in their stalls. Chrissie and I have visited many times before."

"Thanks Elizabeth, I'd love that. Maybe Chrissie and I could get a lesson one day," Becky replied.

"Oh dear," Eva said. "Be careful, Elizabeth, or you'll be creating a rod for our backs. Riding lessons cost a fortune. You'll have to make do with just looking for the time being," she added.

They headed off in the direction of the lake and when they arrived at the jetty, Elizabeth could see Johnny Rigby and Theo Walker climbing into a rowing boat with their sons.

"That's my bosses and their sons," she said and she waved at them and they returned the gesture.

"I'll be okay waiting here on my own for Dad," Chrissie signed. "I don't want him to come along and see everyone standing here. He's due any minute. Please leave Mum. Mr. Rigby and Mr. Walker are here so I'll be fine."

Once again Elizabeth looked at her watch. "Okay, Pet," she said giving Chrissie a kiss. "We'll get going. Have a nice time with your dad. Text me if there's any problem and I'll come right back and get you."

The group wandered off leaving Chrissie waiting at the jetty. Elizabeth kept looking back, but there was no sign of William yet. She felt sure he'd arrive because he hadn't phoned to say anything different. She expected he'd be at least ten minutes late as usual, but with Mr. Rigby and Mr. Walker on the lake and Chrissie having her phone, Elizabeth felt sure she'd be okay.

***

Lionel Goodheart and Stanley Jones had packed their picnic away and taken all their belongings back to the

Home where they'd both changed into suitable attire for the award ceremony. They relished being in the spotlight and wanted to look their best. Each wore cream coloured, linen trousers, a navy blue blazer and a crisply ironed shirt. Goodheart sported a blue tie and Jones a red one.

"Nobody can accuse us of being politically biased," Goodheart said. "Between us we cover both persuasions."

"In every sense," Jones replied and gave a mock smile.

"Indeed," Goodheart agreed. "This occasion really marks the end of an era, don't you think?" He had a rather rueful expression and seemed quite emotional.

"Or the beginning of a better one, perhaps," his friend replied. "Now we have decided to buy Albany House we should start looking for furniture. Our meagre bits and pieces will barely fill three rooms let alone an entire house. We could perhaps visit Milan for ideas. The designers there are said to be top class."

"Or maybe the antique markets of Paris," Goodheart replied, his spirits lifting at the prospect. "Paris is so Bohemian, so exciting and I'm sure we'll discover much more than a few sticks of furniture there. We might even stay for a month. With the rental we'll be receiving for the Home, we'll easily be able to afford it. I never dreamt the Council would pay so much, but they can't afford the home to close so they really have no choice."

The two men walked towards the stage. They

stood at the foot of the stairs as Counsellor Brown made the introduction.

Goodheart smiled benignly and Jones fidgeted in anticipation.

CHAPTER 37

The gunman, dressed in combat gear, swallowed some more pills then walked purposefully to the middle of the grass, amongst the groups of families and friends, amongst the blankets on the ground, the remnants of fried chicken, sandwiches, cakes and soft drinks. No one looked at him or acknowledged him, too busy interacting with their families or friends. He didn't look out of place as many people were clothed in fancy dress costumes. He could have been invisible and he wondered if he was. Smiling to himself, he was eerily calm, but his heart was racing, wired by the drugs he'd been popping all night and all day to help him to stay awake. Raising his automatic weapon, he pirouetted, finger on the trigger, firing indiscriminately into the crowd, whooping and cheering as people collapsed dead or dying. It's just like the fairground, he thought.

Carlo Donatelli lay on his side on the grass. One arm was bent at the elbow and his head was leaning on his hand as he stared adoringly at his beautiful wife. His bright yellow T-shirt had ridden up exposing his podgy midriff. He tugged at it, pulling it down because blades of grass were tickling his belly.

Carlotta sat up, moved into a kneeling position then stretched her arms above her head. "I love you my Italian stallion," she said smiling at the plump little man and he chuckled because he knew that she meant every word and it delighted him.

Carlo heard the thump, thump, thump at the same moment his wife's arms and chest exploded with blood. For a split second he saw her face sag and her eyes roll in their sockets, before she fell backwards onto the grass. He struggled to his knees and reached out for her then the next burst of gunfire cut him down. He was dead before his body hit the ground. His fat little arm lay across Carlotta's ravaged torso and the blood from their gaping wounds turned the green grass, red.

Close by, Bee and Mandy saw them collapse. They didn't know what was happening. People began to scream. As Bee stood up for a better look, a bullet hit her shoulder spinning her round. She sank to her knees, her pallor grey. Mandy crawled towards her and placed her arm protectively across her chest easing her down onto the ground. She stared into her friends eyes.

"Bee, are you okay? Oh, my God, you're bleeding."

She heard the gunman whooping and cheering.

"Emma," Bee managed to say before blacking out.

Mandy lay perfectly still as Bee's blood soaked her clothes. She heard the gunman's boots crunching through the dry grass. He was coming towards her. Terrified, she shut her eyes. The man stood so close to her his foot pinned her hair to the ground and his ankle pressed against her head.

"Where's my prize?" she heard him mutter.

Then he was gone, running towards the stage. She thought about Theo and Charlie and figured they'd already be on the island. They're safe, I'm sure they're safe. Please God, let them be safe.

Mandy inhaled slowly then dared to open her eyes. She could see the gunman walking forward firing his weapon. Praying he wouldn't turn round she quickly made her way towards the marquee. All her thoughts were focussed on saving Emma, Marie and Isobel.

William Black heard the gunfire as he stepped out of his car. He began to run towards the lake. He could see Chrissie looking at the ducks. Not being able to hear, she had no idea what was happening behind her. William reached his daughter, gripped her shoulders and spun her round just as the gunman's bullet ripped through his chest. The same bullet then travelled on grazing Chrissie's head. He pulled her with him as he sank to the ground.

"I love you. Play dead," he managed to mouth as he collapsed over her.

Numb with shock, Chrissie did as she was told. She lay perfectly still and closed her eyes as her father's warm blood soaked into her clothes.

Neil was standing beside the stairs which led to the stage. He was lurking in the shadows waiting for the right moment. He'd waited for years, waited for most of his life to confront his demons, to confront the monster who had nearly destroyed him. Just when Goodheart and Jones were about to receive the award and the local press photographer stood by to capture the moment, he stepped forward to pounce. After all the pain and humiliation he would finally have a voice. He'd expose these awful men for the paedophiles they were. He would ruin them and they'd never again have the chance to damage another child.

At that moment a hail of bullets ripped across the stage and Neil slunk back into the shadows. Goodheart, Jones and Councillor Brown were torn apart, their bodies jerking on the floor as another rain of bullets hit them. Then the gunman turned towards the marquee.

Neil could hear screaming, a raw animal keening. He didn't realise that the awful sound, the terrible screaming of rage and despair was coming from him. He bounded up the stairs to the stage and ran towards the broken, bloody body of Stanley Jones. Pounding on the man's ravaged chest he yelled, "Don't die you bastard, don't you dare die. I want justice. It's too easy if you die."

He broke into loud, desperate sobs, kneeling on the floor he held his head in his hands and rocked back and forth. "Don't die," he cried.

It took Colin a few moments to realise what was happening, but when he did, the shock hit him like a brick.

"Caitlin, Rhona, run!" he screamed. "Run for the trees."

"What trees? Where? Where can we go?" Caitlin cried. "How can we get away? Oh, my God, he's coming. Run, Mum, run."

Grabbing Rhona by the arm Caitlin screamed at

her, "Now, Mum, run."

"Alan, what about Alan? He's in the toilet."

"I'll get him," Colin said. "Run away, now, he's coming, the gunman is coming."

The two women ran towards the line of trees at the side of the park leaving Colin to try to rescue Alan. He banged on the door of the toilet.

"Alan, get out of there. There's a gunman coming. He's shooting people. We have to get away."

"Well that's original," Alan replied, now rather merry from beer and not believing a word of it.

"For God's sake, Alan, hurry, he's coming. We're going to be killed."

The toilet flushed and a bemused Alan opened the door. Unable to comprehend the scene in front of his eyes, he allowed himself to be led by Colin. People were running trying to reach the main exit. They stampeded chaotically, each fearing they were about to die, stumbling over the fallen, trampling on faces, crushing fingers, abandoning friends, in a desperate bid to survive.

Attempting to swim against the tide, Colin half dragged, half carried Alan towards the line of trees. Behind those trees, Colin knew lay a footpath and a gate which would eventually lead them to safety.

More by luck than design, Marie, Isobel and their new boyfriends also ran towards the trees. It was too late to consider Emma as far as Marie was concerned. She might already be dead. It was time to save herself.

Emma stood just inside the entrance of the

marquee. She was completely bewildered, not knowing what she should do. Marie told her not to leave the tent until she came back for her, but everyone else was running away. From where she stood she could hear the sound of the gunfire, she could see people falling down, stumbling and tumbling, hear the screaming and the yelling as they tried to escape.

Suddenly, in front of her, was Mandy. She grabbed Emma by the arm and dragged her back inside the tent.

"We can't go that way," she explained, pointing towards the doorway. "There's a bad man coming and we have to run away."

Quickly Mandy appraised their position. The only way to escape, the only safe place, was through the back of the marquee, but there was no exit. Mandy searched all round the edge of the canvas where it touched the ground. It was pegged down tight. Finally, she discovered a small space, where two canvas sheets were incorrectly laced. A tiny space a child might fit through. With all her strength, Mandy tugged at the material to enlarge the hole.

"Here, Emma, try to crawl through this space and when you get outside don't run towards the gate, run towards the trees and don't look back."

Emma froze. She was scared.

"Now Emma, move it," Mandy screamed.

As the child wriggled through the tiny space, Mandy heard the gunfire draw nearer.

"Run," she screamed, "Run."

Mandy let go of the canvas. There was no way

she could escape through the tiny hole. As she turned the gunman entered the marquee. Everyone else had fled. She was alone with the shooter.

"Please," she begged, "Please, I have a son."

"Yes, you do," the man replied.

Mandy was crying. She squinted through the tears. "You," she said recognising the man who stood before her. "Why?" she asked.

The gunman rested his AK-47 on the ground, reaching for a handgun he shot Mandy. The bullet blew a hole in her shoulder and she collapsed to the ground.

"Because I can," he replied.

***

When Danny Frankel entered the park he had no idea what he was going to do or say. With his business on the line, his father turning his back on him and only a few copper coins to his name, he'd finally reached rock bottom. Now the only way was up. After arriving home from his fruitless trip to his father's house, Danny tidied himself up. He washed, shaved then dressed in clean, smart casual wear. He knew the Donatellis and the Walkers would probably be attending Rigby's charity event and he needed to speak to Carlo and Phil. He had to try to rescue his order and in doing so save his company.

When Danny walked onto the grass he was surrounded by utter devastation. People were screaming and crying, dead or dying. He could smell their blood. An overwhelming coppery taste filled his mouth. Shocked, he stumbled forward. When he came across the bodies of the Donatellis he despaired. Danny had never had to be brave. He had no idea what he was capable of because someone always helped him, someone always bailed him out of trouble. Now he found himself following a deranged gunman, determined to stop him.

As Eddie Maxwell stepped out of the marquee, Danny Frankel was there. With no thought of his own safety, Danny launched himself at Eddie and both men fell to the ground. The AK-47 fell from Eddie's grasp, but he still gripped the Glock. The men wrestled and rolled on the grass both struggling for control of the weapon. As they fought they could hear the sounds of approaching emergency vehicles.

"Give it up. It's over," Danny gasped, with his strength almost gone.

With a mighty effort, Eddie forced the gun between their grappling bodies. His finger was pressed on the trigger. Over and over bullets spewed from the weapon tearing into both men, in seconds the hero and the madman lay dead.

Later, when the news broke and Victor was informed of his son's death, he wept. Danny had only performed one selfless act in his entire life and it had cost him his life. Now, finally, Victor had a son to be proud of.

Mandy and Bee both survived their injuries, but their friendship never fully recovered. How could anyone or anything ever be the same again?

William died saving Chrissie finally deserving the pedestal she'd placed him upon. His brave and selfless act a constant reminder to Elizabeth of the man she'd fallen in love with all those years before.

Fourteen people were slaughtered that day and over forty were injured, but many more lives were changed forever. Some people became heroes while others were destroyed. The massacre touched every family. The picnic at Presley Park would never be forgotten. Even years after the event, people would talk about it in shocked whispers remembering the horror of that fateful day.

Do you sometimes wonder how you'd behave in a crisis, if your life was on the line, if you were facing imminent death? Would you stop to help a stranger? Would you save your wife, your husband, your parents your children? Perhaps a mother would save her child. But perhaps not.

END

Massacre at Presley Park

Other books by Elly Grant –
From the Death in the Pyrenees series

'Palm Trees in the Pyrenees' is the first book in Elly Grant's series 'Death in the Pyrenees'.
The story unfolds, told by Danielle a single, downtrodden , thirty year old, who is the only cop in the small Pyrenean town. She feels unappreciated and unnoticed, having been passed over for promotion in favour of her male colleagues working in the region. But everything is about to change. The sudden and mysterious death of a much hated locally based Englishman will have far reaching affects.

'Grass Grows in the Pyrenees' is the second book in Elly Grant's series 'Death in the Pyrenees'.
The story unfolds, told by Danielle, a single, thirty year old, recently promoted cop. The sudden and mysterious death of a local farmer suspected of growing cannabis, opens a 'Pandora's' box of trouble. It's a race against time to stop the gangsters before the town, and everyone in it, is damaged beyond repair

'Red light in the Pyrenees' is the third book in Elly Grant's series 'Death in the Pyrenees'.
The story unfolds, told by Danielle, a single, thirty-something, respected, female cop. The sudden and violent death of a local Madame brings fear to her working girls and unsettles the town. But doesn't every

cloud have a silver lining? Danielle follows the twists and turns of events until a surprising truth is revealed. Hold your breath, it's a bumpy ride.

'Dead End in the Pyrenees' is the fourth book in Elly Grant's series 'Death in the Pyrenees'.
The story unfolds, told by Danielle, a single, thirty-something, highly respected, female cop. A sudden and unexpected death at the local spa brings to light other mysterious deaths. Important local people are involved, people who Danielle respects. She must quickly solve the case before things get out of control

'Deadly Degrees in the Pyrenees' is the fifth book in Elly Grant's series 'Death in the Pyrenees'.
The story unfolds, told by Danielle, a single, thirty-something, senior, female cop. The ghastly murder of a local estate agent reveals unscrupulous business deals. Danielle's friends may be in danger. She must catch the killer before anyone else is harmed

All these stories are about life in a small French town, local events, colourful characters, prejudice and of course, death.

Also by Elly Grant
The Unravelling of Thomas Malone

The mutilated corpse of a young prostitute is discovered in a squalid apartment.

Angela Murphy has recently started working as a detective on the mean streets of Glasgow. Just days into the job she's called to attend this grisly murder. She is shocked by the horror of the scene. It's a ghastly sight of blood and despair.

To her boss, Frank Martin, there's something horribly familiar about the scene.
Is this the work of a copycat killer?
Will he strike again?
With limited resources and practically no experience, Angela is desperate to prove herself.
But is her enthusiasm sufficient?
Can she succeed before the killer strikes again?

The Coming of the Lord

Breaking the Thomas Malone case was an achievement but nothing could prepare DC Angela Murphy or her colleagues for the challenge ahead.
Escaped psychopathic sociopath John Baptiste, is big, powerful and totally out of control. Guided by his

perverse religious interpretation of morality, he wreaks havoc.

An under-resourced police department struggles to cope, not only with this new threat, but also the ruthless antics of ganglord Jackie McGeachy.

Pressure mounts along with the body count.

Glasgow has never felt more dangerous.

Never Ever Leave Me

'Never Ever Leave Me ' is a modern romance

Katy Bradley had a perfect life, or so she thought. Perfect husband, perfect job and a perfect home until one day, one awful day when everything fell apart. Full of fear and dread, Katy had no choice but to run, but would her split-second decision carry her forward to safety or back to the depths of despair? A chance encounter with a handsome stranger gives her hope. Never ever leave me, sees Katy trapped between two worlds, her future and her past. Will she have the strength to survive? Will she ever find happiness again?

Released by Elly Grant Together with Angi Fox

But Billy Can't Fly

At over six feet tall, blonde and blue-eyed, Billy looks like an Adonis, but he is simple minded, not the full shilling, one slice less than a sandwich, not quite right in the head. When you meet him you might not notice at first, but after a couple of minutes it becomes apparent. The lights are on but nobody's home. In Billy's mind, he's Superman, a righter of wrongs, a saver of souls and that's where it all goes wrong. He interacts with the people he meets at a bus stop, Jez, a rich public schoolboy, Melanie the office slut, Bella Worthington, the leader of the local W.I. and David, a gay, Jewish teacher. This book moves quickly along as each character tells their part of the tale. Billy's story is darkly funny, poignant and tragic. Full of stereotypical prejudices, it offends on every level, but is difficult to put down.

Released by Elly Grant Together with Zach Abrams

Twists and Turns

With fear, horror, death and despair, these stories will surprise you, scare you and occasionally make you smile. Twists & Turns offer the reader thought provoking tales. Whether you have a minute to spare or an hour or more, open Twists & Turns for a world full of mystery, murder, revenge and intrigue. A unique collaboration by the authors Elly Grant and Zach Abrams

About the author

Hi, my name is Elly Grant and I like to kill people. I use a variety of methods. Some I drop from a great height, others I drown, but I've nothing against suffocation, stabbing, poisoning or simply battering a person to death. As long as it grabs my reader's attention, I'm satisfied.

I've written several novels and short stories. My series 'Death in the Pyrenees' comprises, 'Palm Trees in the Pyrenees,' 'Grass Grows in the Pyrenees,' 'Red Light in the Pyrenees', 'Dead End in the Pyrenees' and 'Deadly Degrees in the Pyrenees'. They are all set in a small town in France. These novels are published by Author Way Limited. Author Way has also published, 'The Unravelling of Thomas Malone' as well as a collaboration of short stories called 'Twists and Turns'.

As I live much of my life in a small French town in the Eastern Pyrenees, I get inspiration from the way of life and the colourful characters I come across. I don't have to search very hard to find things to write about and living in the most prolific wine producing region in France makes the task so much more delightful.

Perhaps you will visit my town one day. Perhaps you will sit near me in a café or return my smile as I walk past you in the street. Perhaps you will hold my interest for a while, and maybe, just maybe, you will be my next victim. But don't concern yourself too much, because, at least for the time being, I always manage to confine my murderous ways to paper.

Read books from the 'Death in the Pyrenees' series, enter my small French town and meet some of the people who live there ----- and die there.

Alternatively read about life on some of the toughest streets in Glasgow or for something more varied delve into my short stories.

To contact Elly, mailto: ellygrant@authorway.net

About Author Way Limited

Author Way provides a broad range of good quality, previously unpublished works and makes them available to the public on multiple formats.

We have a fast growing number of authors who have completed or are in the process of completing their books and preparing them for publication and these will shortly be available.

Please keep checking our website to hear about the latest developments.

Author Way Limited

www.authorway.net

Made in the USA
Charleston, SC
05 January 2015